ten hours to live

'Once I started reading I couldn't stop'
– letter from a fourteen-year-old boy

Pete Johnson says this is his 'most personal work'.

Pete says, 'I wanted to write a love story from the point of view of a boy. I wished to delve into the traumas of unrequited love – but with a humorous touch. The only way I could do this was by drawing on my own life. Ben's mistakes are mine. He is the nearest I have ever come to a self-portrait.'

Pete Johnson has been a film extra, a film critic for Radio 1, an English teacher and a journalist. However, his dream was always to be a writer. At the age of ten he wrote a fan letter to Dodie Smith, author of *The Hundred and One Dalmations*, and together they communicated for many years. Dodie Smith was the first person to encourage him to be a writer.

He has written many books for children as well as plays for the theatre and Radio 4, and is a popular visitor to schools and libraries.

Some other books by Pete Johnson

THE PROTECTORS
MIND READER: BLACKMAIL

For Younger Readers

BUG BROTHER
PIRATE BROTHER

ten hours to live

PETE JOHNSON

PUFFIN BOOKS

PUFFIN BOOKS

Published by the Penguin Group
Penguin Books Ltd, 80 Strand, London, WC2R 0RL, England
Penguin Putnam Inc., 375 Hudson Street, New York, New York 10014, USA
Penguin Books Australia Ltd, 250 Camberwell Road, Camberwell, Victoria 3124, Australia
Penguin Books Canada Ltd, 10 Alcorn Avenue, Toronto, Ontario, Canada M4V 3B2
Penguin Books India (P) Ltd, 11 Community Centre, Panchsheel Park, New Delhi – 110 017, India
Penguin Books (NZ) Ltd, Cnr Rosedale and Airborne Roads, Albany, Auckland, New Zealand
Penguin Books (South Africa) (Pty) Ltd, 24 Sturdee Avenue, Rosebank 2196, South Africa

Penguin Books Ltd, Registered Offices: 80 Strand, London WC2R 0RL, England

www.penguin.com

First published by Mammoth, an imprint of Egmont Children's Books Limited 1995
Published in Puffin Books 2002
1

Set in 11.5/17.5 pt Goudy
Typeset by Rowland Phototypesetting Ltd, Bury St Edmunds, Suffolk
Made and printed in England by Clays Ltd, St Ives plc

British Library Cataloguing in Publication Data

A CIP catalogue record for this book is available from the British Library

ISBN 0–141–31422–2

. . . And every love is a screen for sadness –
          Salvatore Quasimodo

Ten Hours to Live

I'm a prisoner waiting to be sentenced.

I was up before six o'clock this morning. I couldn't sleep. This was judgement day.

I did my hair, picked my clothes with special care, brushed my teeth ten times. Then I prepared the house. I worked out where she'll sit, where I'll sit. Then I hoovered and tidied up. I even went round straightening the pictures. For a while I was busy, purposeful. But now there is nothing left to do – except wait.

This is such agony.

I feel as if I'm totally at her mercy. I hate that feeling.

I keep going into the kitchen and making tea. I enjoy doing that. It's just the product I'm not too keen on. My tea tastes horrible today. I'm building up quite a collection of mugs of tea. Somewhere there's some toast, too.

I did try and chill out in my bedroom. I put on some of my favourite tapes. Normally, I can listen to good music for hours. But today, nothing reaches me. All I can do is stare out of my window. I know I shouldn't do this. She'll never come if I watch for her. People never do.

Outside it's building up to be another July scorcher, yet it seems more like a Sunday than a Friday. It's eerie. There's a supermarket down the road but I can't see any mums out with their prams, no children, no old people off to get Pedigree Chum for their dogs. Perhaps I'm the only person left alive.

Anything's possible today. It's as if everything's just stopped. The whole world is waiting to see if . . .

Only on my telly screen is life going on as normal. Nothing can stop morning television. If the end of the world was announced those same faces would still pop up telling you all the things you can do with a kiwi fruit. I've switched the volume down low. I don't want to hear what they're saying, but I need some noise around me.

And the telly serves as a kind of visual clock. I can measure out my day in television programmes. Now the faces are becoming more earnest and serious, so it must be time for the local news. I start to imagine my story up there. 'And there's still no news from Ben Chaplin's house, where he is anxiously waiting for Miss Sophie Doyle. Ben, how do you feel about this?'

'Chuffed to bits. How do you think?'

'Yes, well, Ben's obviously rather upset. So I think we'll go back to the studio for our lead story: woman falls over a bag of oranges. Here's an action replay.'

But suddenly, I call the reporter back. 'Before you go, will you broadcast this message? Sophie, why are you spinning it out like this? Don't make me play the waiting game any more. Just come round, will you? COME ROUND.'

You see, I still don't know how it happened.

I said something very stupid, which I regretted instantly. But I said it because I was hurt. I didn't mean anything by it. And I've spent a week apologising for my foolishness.

It was one week ago tonight when Sophie ran out on me. Now I'm not welcome at her house (apparently) and she refuses to speak to me on the phone.

And all I want to do is apologise properly to her.

But that's quite hard to do when someone won't come to the door, and slams the phone down on you. So I apologised to her over six sides of my mum's writing pad and then I invited her to sit round the negotiating table with me. I didn't put it like that, of course. I told her that

3

I was still alone in my house. I've been on my own here for over a week now, ever since Mum was rushed into hospital because of high blood pressure; one of the dangers of a woman of her age having a baby. She'd been let out of hospital to go to Aunt Annie's for a good rest. She and Dad and Glen, my six-year-old brother, are still there. Yesterday, on the phone, Dad hinted that Mum might stay there until the baby is born; it's due in about ten days time.

I was invited to Aunt Annie's as well. But I told them I was needed at the video shop. That was my pretend reason for staying on here. Actually, I'm supposed to be doing an eight-hour shift at the video shop today. But I phoned in sick. I couldn't step out of this house for eight minutes, let alone eight hours.

I've asked Sophie to come round – please – or at least ring some time today. I didn't want to put any pressure on her, so the time she called was entirely up to her. I'll wait in all day, if necessary. I don't care. I just want this to be sorted. And the only way it can be sorted is if we speak.

Please, please call me next Friday. That's what I wrote at the end of my letter. Then I read it over about a thousand times. I disguised my writing on the envelope. I didn't want her chucking it away without reading it. Finally I posted it. Later I went back to the post-box to check it had gone down properly. I didn't want my letter jammed somewhere getting soggy, my words all smudged.

I'm actually a lousy letter-writer. In the past when I had pen-friends in Germany, or somewhere, I always intended to write them interesting letters – in my head they were great – but they always turned out bland and dull. In fact, I was always surprised when anyone answered back.

Perhaps I don't like putting my feelings on paper for all the world to see. Sophie's letter was different. And without sounding vain, I was quite proud of it. For once, I'd risked exposing my feelings. And unless you had a heart of steel, I don't think you could have ignored it. To be honest, I was expecting Sophie to race round to my house. That's why I was up so early.

Instead, she's just left me hanging here.

That's beyond cruel. I couldn't have done that to someone I cared about, to anyone, in fact. I didn't think Sophie could either. Three days before the break-up Sophie said to me, 'You don't know how much I care about you.' What I don't understand is how could she say that – and I believe she really meant it – and then do this to me. It doesn't make any sense. Especially as we were so close. That's why, all week, I've been trying to get some telepathy going. Somehow, I must be able to pick up what's wrong.

If only I knew what she was doing now. Maybe she's out somewhere, having a good time, not even thinking about me. I like to torment myself with that thought. It works every time, too. But of course she's thinking about me. Unless these last months have been a total illusion . . . No, that isn't possible. I know what she's doing: she's staring into her mirror going over what she's going to say to me when she comes round. She's probably been rehearsing all morning. I wonder if she's got as many speeches as me. Here's one I made earlier.

I imagine the phone ringing. And I just let it ring for a while. Then I pick it up, cool and relaxed. She's just another friend calling. I tell her all the things I've done (all made up). My casualness is wounding. And I want to wound her for prolonging my agony like this. But I know I'll never do it.

I think I've gone through every scenario, every conversation we could possibly have, including a very dangerous one. Late at night, when I can't sleep, I unlock my heart to her. I tell her I'll make any concessions she wants. I'll agree to anything, sign anything, if she'll just come back. Because, without her, my life is worthless.

It pains me to hear that speech, for what am I doing, but begging. And you should never let anyone catch you doing that. For then they've got you by the short and curlies: and don't they know it. I make a promise to myself, that whatever happens, this last speech will remain my dark secret.

About an hour ago the phone gave a sharp, high-pitched squeak and started ringing. I was up like a shot and, wham, straight down those stairs.

Of course it wasn't Sophie. I'd expected this. As I flew down the stairs I told myself, this will be the false alarm, obligatory in these kind of situations. Still, at least I'd got it out of the way. And I knew for certain the phone was working. (I'd been worrying about that all morning.)

Besides, it was lucky Sophie hadn't rung then, because when I picked up the receiver I did something incredibly stupid. In an effort to be easy and normal, I said, '716282.' It was only when I'd finished I realised that it was Sophie's number I'd been reciting.

'You sad muppet,' said Simon. He laughed. I laughed. We were both horribly embarrassed. Simon was ringing from Jenny's house. They were the only people – apart from Sophie – who knew about today's ordeal. Jenny came on the line too. They both did their best to cheer me up and show solidarity. I really appreciated that. Yet, all the time I couldn't help wondering, what if Sophie's trying to get through now.

Quick time-check: the Australian soaps are taking

over the airways, so it's early afternoon, twoish. How many more hours must I wait like this? Simon reckons she'll make a dramatic late-night appearance. So I could be waiting here for another nine or ten hours. Ten hours.

I've got ten hours to live.

What a strange thing to write, as if I'm about to die. I'm eighteen not eighty. I should have decades ahead of me.

But do you want to know the truth? I can't see beyond today. Nothing else exists.

I mean, in June I sat my A levels and it was quite a big deal. But I tell you, if someone rushed in here and said, 'Ben, here are your exam grades, two weeks early, you've passed all three with grade As,' I'd just say, 'Yes, but when's Sophie going to ring?'

My life contains only her, which is a bit of a downer when she's nowhere to be found.

WHERE IS SOPHIE?

Why is this all I can think about? All I care about. I don't like what's happening to me. I'm changing into someone I despise: someone who writes pathetic things like, I've got ten hours to live. This isn't me. It's as if I've been put under a spell.

Yes, that's it: Sophie's bewitched me.

How did she do that?

If I knew that, maybe I could break the spell, get some

power back. Somehow, I've got to make sense of this. The only way I can do that is by going back. I must call Sophie out of the past.

10 . . . Just a Dream

So where do I begin. How about last October, the first time I met Sophie. No, I'd pictured her in my head long before that. That's where my story really starts. You could say she bewitched me before I even met her.

My soul mate.

When I first heard the legend that our souls were flying above our heads searching for the perfect partner, so they could link together and be one, I thought it seemed eerie. I didn't like the idea of these flying souls at all. They sounded like bats.

The legend also stated that until we found our soul mate, our life would be incomplete. The good news was, that everyone has one. Apparently, our soul mates are out there. Why was it whenever people talked about soul mates and aliens, they always referred to them as being 'out there'? Maybe you were as likely to meet your soul mate as an alien.

And what if your soul mate was born in 1066 or lived in Outer Mongolia? Hard luck, I suppose. Yet, I still believed there was something in the idea. After all, millions of people have found soul-mate-type partners. Why shouldn't I?

I looked forward to meeting this special girl. I'd imagine her sometimes: not so much what she looked like, as what it would be like to meet a person with whom I had such a special connection. I'd had a hint of things to come from Simon and Jenny, my only friends who were on the same wavelength as me and whom I could trust totally. We'd known each other since we were thirteen. Then, when we were sixteen, there might have been a major parting of the ways. I stayed on at school to do A levels, while Simon left to do a three-year course at college, Jenny to change jobs almost weekly. Yet the friendship, the bond between us, remained as strong as ever. After that, I thought we were invincible.

Everyone was intrigued by our friendship: one girl going around with two guys, hey-hey! Actually, I suppose Jenny was a kind of substitute girlfriend for both Simon and me. She'd pay us compliments, flirt with us, even act all huffy when either of us was seeing a girl. 'So I'm not enough for you, am I? I've got to share you with someone else,' she'd say. But there was just the tiniest hint that she wasn't totally pretending. It was exciting. So I'd say to her, 'Jenny, you'll always be my top girl.' Simon would chant it too. After which, she'd give a kind of purr of satisfaction: 'And just don't forget it, all right.'

And no doubt about it. Jenny really was my 'top girl'.

There were other girls, of course. But I'd never been in a major relationship, the longest lasted for four months. Sometimes girls finished with me; other times I'd finish it. And by doing that I might have upset a girl or two, unfortunately. They'd liked me, fancied me, they were sad it was over. But I've always remained on speaking terms with my exs. Often we've stayed friends. You might say that's a measure of my failure because I've never really disturbed anyone. No girl's stalked my house weeping, 'I can't live without you.' And no girl's ever come up to me – as they did to this guy in my class – crying, 'I don't care if you're going out with someone else, I'll be second-best.' I remember watching that scene with amazement, sadness for the girl (the guy was a muppet) and deep, deep envy. I had a much better personality than that guy, yet girls got over me quite lightly.

That isn't to say girls don't like me. Sometimes I'll be at a party and I'll turn and see a girl staring at me. Then

I'll catch her eye and she knows she should look away but she doesn't want to. And neither do I. That's one thing I really love. Attraction, in the beginning anyway, is always exciting. It lifts you right up. Suddenly, you're the special person you always hoped you were. It's a massive ego-trip, of course. But it's also really positive.

I'll go over and talk to her. Sometimes she'll have heard about me from one of her friends. I'm pretty well known locally, I guess. I'll make her laugh. She'll see I'm fairly intelligent and, when my hair's slicked back, not bad-looking . . . anything else? Oh yes, girls often say I'm different. It's a compliment and yet it's not. The truth is, if a girl's looking at me, she's on the rebound. Usually she's gone out with some moron for two hundred years and, finally, she's had enough. She wants to meet a guy who's nice and funny and thoughtful. And that's my cue. Not that I see myself as Mr Nice Guy.

I have a quite different image of myself. It's a bit embarrassing, really. When I was about six I read a book (which I've still got) about King Arthur and his trusty Knights of the Round Table. Soon I had a toy sword, a shield, plastic armour, even a knight's helmet. I'd pretend my bedroom was a castle and all day I'd be hurtling up and down the stairs, charging into walls . . . and as soon as I'd strapped on my plastic armour I thought that I was invincible.

As I got older I reluctantly put away the toy sword and the plastic armour but I never really grew out of it. I read book after book about King Arthur's knights. I live in their world where damsels were rescued from fiery dragons.

Then sometimes I'd be with a girl in the town centre on a Friday night where all around us guys were celebrating the end of another great night by emptying the contents of their stomach on to the pavement. Everything seemed so shabby and pointless that I'd say to the girl beside me, 'Come on then, command me, good lady. What noble deed can I perform for you?'

She'd laugh (sometimes quite nervously) but I'd continue in that role for quite a while, gushing all this stuff I'd read at her. And occasionally, she would command me to do something. Well, once this girl's friend had left her coat inside a pub and was scared to get it back because her ex-boyfriend was in there.

'Good lady, what does death matter if I can serve you,' I said, before charging into the pub. I actually retrieved the coat without any trouble. So it wasn't really much of a noble deed. Still, my act (and that's all it was really) intrigued a number of girls and, as I said, they thought I was funny and different and nice. But actually, they missed the point of it.

Only one person really understood what I was going

on about. I've not only kept the card Sophie sent me, but the envelope too. It's here beside me now. On the envelope, Sophie's written: *To Sir Lancelot.*

I did rescue you, didn't I, Sophie? It's strange to think how I met her. Especially as the weeks before I met Sophie were rather grim. For a start, I'd had a bombshell. Simon told me he'd asked Jenny out and she'd accepted. And he looked so uncomfortable when he was telling me that I couldn't help feeling sorry for him.

I didn't want to think about it at first. Then we both tried to make a joke of it all. Simon said they probably wouldn't last for more than one date. By the time Simon left I was sick and scared and angry. The three of us were a team. We were all equal. But now, suddenly, the rules of the game had been changed and without any consultation: now it was them and me. No wonder every time I saw them I felt stranded, alone. And I'll confess something else: deep down I'd always hoped that Jenny liked me better than Simon. Now I knew differently.

I hardly saw Simon and Jenny over the next few weeks, instead, I made myself very busy. I got a job at the local video shop, spent much more time with the sixth-form drama group; played football again on Sunday mornings. I even started handing my A-level essays in on time. But there was still a spare hour or two, so I decided to get fit at the local sports centre. And you might say that's when fate took a hand in my life. For it was there I met Nick Doyle, Sophie's brother.

9 . . . Enter Sophie

Nick was a new guy in our sixth form. I'd spotted him around school, but we weren't doing any of the same A levels so I'd never really spoken to him until we met at the sports centre. We got talking and went for a drink afterwards.

Nick, like me, was tall and skinny but he had very curly dark hair and one of those round, open faces which give the impression you can see everything someone is thinking. If it weren't for his height you'd have thought Nick was younger than he was. But that was what I liked about him. He was light-hearted, and funny, and always wanted to be off somewhere.

He'd recently passed his driving test and his parents had given him a clapped-out red Fiesta, that sounded as if it had a hole in the exhaust. Sometimes we'd drive half the night in that car: me, his 'co-pilot', poring over the map in search of some obscure landscape. Somehow, we always ended up at Luton airport. And every time we went there we were in disguise. Our favourite was as undercover men for the SAS waiting to intercept someone very dangerous. Nick called himself Monty and for some mysterious reason always spoke like Sean Connery. I dubbed myself Carruthers and was terribly British. We could spend hours talking total rubbish to each other. That's my biggest memory of Nick now; he and I saying things like, 'Monty, I thought you ought to know, you smell.'

'Decent of you to tell me, Carruthers.'

On the page, now, not funny at all. Yet at the time, we'd just be killing ourselves. And on the way home Nick would tell jokes. Only he never got to the punchline, because he would be laughing so much. The car would swerve this way and that, I'd be half-shouting, half-laughing at him and he'd be shaking, actually shaking with laughter.

He was just a big kid. And in many ways he was surprisingly naive and clumsy. He used to wear white socks (!) and the most rank trainers you've ever seen. You could say I became his mentor, advising him on everything, from his clothes to his love life.

He was mad about Vanessa, a girl at our school, but too shy to say anything. He blushed if she was in the same room as him. I was persuaded to talk to her on his behalf, as I saw her after school at drama. I never told Nick, but at first Vanessa wasn't interested in him at all. 'He's just so immature,' she said. And really, I couldn't see them together. Vanessa was quite pretty: short blonde hair, very curvy lips, and a way of suddenly gazing up at you, all rapt attention, that was very flattering. Yet, she dressed like a thirty-five-year-old mum: in her nice little blouses and jeans. And sometimes she acted like a thirty-five-year-old mum. She never messed about. She couldn't see the point of it. So she wasn't exactly an ideal companion for Nick She was also a terrible snob.

I remember her going to a party once and declaring, 'I hate houses where there's no hallway and the stairs are right in front of you.' A lot of people hated her for saying that. She's been trying to live down that crack ever since. I played on this by saying to her, 'I told Nick he hasn't got a chance with you, his house is far too small.'

'Oh, you didn't say that,' she cried.

'Yeah, I said Vanessa will think your house is the shed.'

'You really make me sound horrible and I'm not like that, really, I'm not.'

I didn't reply. I just raised a sceptical eyebrow. Then I slipped in a comment about Nick's deep but totally hopeless love for her.

She smiled and said, 'You do talk such rubbish.'

But I knew I was starting to hook her. Soon I'd persuaded her to send Nick a little message. He was very excited by this note (even though it was pretty dull) and was full of praise for me, his matchmaker. To my surprise, I was quite enjoying the whole thing: courting a girl for someone else was quite creative, really.

And then Nick introduced me to his sister.

It was a Wednesday night and I'd just arrived at Nick's house when the phone rang. He told me to go on through to the lounge and he'd be there in a minute. I'd thought the lounge would be empty but when I opened the door there was Sophie, sitting in one of their huge armchairs, her arms wrapped around herself as if she was very cold.

She was gazing at the television and I felt awkward. I shuffled over to another of the big armchairs. I hoped Nick wouldn't be long. Then she said, her eyes still on the screen, 'Are you Ben?'

'That's right,' I mumbled. 'And you must be Sophie.'

'Yes.' She looked across at me. She had quite long, shiny black hair, and large green eyes. She was much more attractive than I'd expected. All Nick had told me about her was that she was fifteen. She looked much older.

Then Nick burst in. 'We're watching *Star Trek*,' and he switched the television over.

'I don't particularly want to watch *Star Trek* . . .' I began. But Sophie was already standing up. She'd gone before I finished my sentence.

It's weird to rewind that first meeting with Sophie now and see how quick it all was. It was just a glimpse really, a snapshot. And I exchanged exactly eleven words with her, the person who would turn my life upside down.

'Got to show her who's boss,' said Nick. Then he added, almost proudly, 'She's not bad-looking, is she?'

'No, she isn't,' I agreed.

'She went out with one of my mates once, so be careful.' He was still smiling but his tone was serious.

Then Nick's mum was standing in the doorway. She was very thin with tight, grey hair and large worried eyes. She always seemed as if she had really bad nerves. Just looking at her made you feel tense.

'Good evening, Ben,' she said.

'Good evening, Mrs Doyle,' I replied.

She turned to Nick. 'Sophie's just gone out.'

Nick shrugged his shoulders.

'I heard the door go,' his mum went on. 'Did she tell you where she was going?'

'Not a word,' said Nick.

'She shouldn't just go out like that,' declared his mum. 'I'm sick of you two treating this place like a hotel.'

'Don't pick on me,' said Nick. 'It's Sophie you should be having a go at.'

Nick's dad appeared; he beamed around at us. He was tall and balding and red-faced. He had a strangely empty face. All I could see in it was this desperate desire to be liked.

'Sophie's gone out without a word to anyone,' announced Nick's mum.

'She shouldn't do that,' he said, mildly. 'So what are you lads watching then?'

'*Star Trek*,' replied Nick. 'It's just started.'

'*Star Trek*.' Nick's dad considered this news carefully. '*Star Trek*, mmm ... used to watch those when they first came out ... Mmm.' Nick's dad would often hover in the doorway, ask us what we were watching and then do his impression of a reflective bluebottle, before retreating again. Most of the time Nick used to ignore his parents. He seemed to have a strange kind of contempt for them, while his attitude to Sophie shocked me. Especially the night she was taken ill. Nick's parents were out when Sophie stumbled into the kitchen.

'Are there any aspirins?' she gasped. She looked

deathly white. 'It's just, I've got this really bad headache.' She had one of those shaky voices which had a little tremor in it. Nick immediately started to impersonate it. 'It's just I've got this really bad headache,' he mimicked, looking at me. But I didn't smile in return.

'She looks really bad,' I muttered.

Nick hesitated. I think if I hadn't been there he might have helped. But to him, helping Sophie meant losing face. So he turned away from her.

Then I remembered. 'You've got some aspirins in your room, I saw them.' And all at once I became enraged. Someone was in pain, for goodness sake. This wasn't the time for petty squabbles. So I tore up to his room, pulled the bottle of aspirins out of his drawer and dashed back downstairs again.

'Oh, great,' cried Sophie, when she saw them. 'You've saved my life, Ben.' She said this quite lightly, but she was staring right at me. It was also the second time she'd ever said my name, then she disappeared upstairs. There was an awkward silence.

Finally, Nick said, 'You didn't have to give her the whole bottle. I'll never see them again.'

My scalp tightened. 'If it's that important, I'll buy you another bottle tomorrow.'

'Look, just calm down, will you,' said Nick. 'I don't know what you're getting so worked up about.'

I didn't exactly know either. But I stormed out of that house.

I was angry with Nick, certainly, but it wasn't just that. To be honest, I was starting to get a bit bored with him. Going around with him had been like taking a little holiday from my real life. But now I was getting restless. I wanted to go home and home meant, Simon and Jenny. I still saw them of course but only because they made a point of coming into the video shop.

Later that night I decided I'd over-reacted. You have to take people on their own terms. And in his way, Nick was a good bloke. It's just where his sister was concerned he got jealous very easily. I had a feeling the next time I went round Nick's house it would be embarrassing for both of us. But instead, I returned in triumph.

For next day, after drama, Vanessa finally cracked. She told me she was sick of all these notes and messages passing between her and Nick. Why didn't he just take her out for a meal and put an end to all this nonsense. 'He'll have to ring me and arrange it. I'm not doing that,' she said.

'No, sure, that's fine,' I said.

I was really proud of myself. Then I wondered how the real Nick – as opposed to the one I'd created for Vanessa's benefit – would get on. I expected their date would be a disaster. Still, at least Nick would get his chance.

If nothing else, he'd have one date with his dream girl.

When I told Nick, I really thought he was going to cry. Then he insisted I stand next to him while he made the phone call. I'd already coached him on what to say. He followed my speech word for word. Afterwards, his voice was incredulous, as he told me, 'She said to pick her up at eight o'clock on Saturday . . . I really didn't think she liked me. I don't know how you did it . . .' He made me feel like some kind of magician.

To my surprise, he then went into the kitchen to tell his mum, with me posted beside him. His mum raised both hands in the air when he told her. At first I thought she was going to sing. But instead, she just kept saying, 'I'm so pleased, so pleased,' and I really think she was. Then she made this massive plateful of chicken sandwiches and told me to eat as many as I wanted.

Later Nick's dad emerged from his greenhouse (where he used to go for a crafty smoke, apparently) to join the festivities. He stood smiling at us across the kitchen.

Even Sophie made an appearance. 'Well, you're certainly the hero of the house tonight.' She said this quite lightly, rather as she'd said, 'You saved my life,' when I gave her the aspirins.

'Yeah, that's me,' I replied in the same light tone. 'Sir Lancelot, at your service.'

'Sir Lancelot,' she repeated, only quite slowly, as if she

was thinking about it. Then she smiled at me. A wide, generous smile. And for the first time I noticed a little gap between her two front teeth. I liked that tiny imperfection. It made her seem more attractive, somehow.

8 . . . Sophie's Matchmaker

Surely no car ever gleamed and shone the way Nick's did before his first date with Vanessa. We'd spent all afternoon on it.

'She may be bored out of her mind and think I'm a total geek, but at least she can't say my car is dirty,' said Nick.

Just before he left he said to me, 'I wish you were coming as well.'

'You don't need me,' I said. 'Just remember the golden rule: everyone likes talking about themselves. You'll be great.'

But I couldn't help wondering how he would get on without me.

Next morning he rang me, convinced he'd blown it.

She was even more wonderful than he'd expected: they'd even had a laugh together. But he never asked her for another date. 'Without your words I was nothing,' he said.

Then to my surprise Vanessa rang me. She wanted to know if I'd spoken to Nick.

'Yeah, just a few minutes ago, actually. He thought you were great.'

'Really, is that what he said?' She was trying to be cool but not succeeding. 'I was afraid I'd be a let-down. He'd built me up so much . . . I was quite nervous, actually.'

Funny, I hadn't reckoned on Vanessa being nervous. She told me how she'd sent her chips flying on to Nick's plate and he was so witty about it all . . . she raved on and on until she said, 'Don't tell Nick, but last night I had the strangest dream about him. I was arguing with my stepdad, just for a change, when my mum came up, shook me by the hand and said, "I agree with everything you say, but you know you'll have to leave home now." I was so upset, until I looked round and saw Nick standing beside me. And I only saw him for a second but it was like he changed everything.'

It was then I knew Nick was home and dry. For, if you dream about someone, it means one thing: you've let that person get inside your head. And if your dream is like Vanessa's, then it's just as if you've swallowed a love potion. You're hooked.

Nick and Vanessa insisted I go out with them for a drink the next evening. Strange how quickly match-makers can become redundant; one of the hazards of the profession, I suppose. At one point Nick and Vanessa were kissing each other for so long the barman nudged me and asked, 'Are those two coming up for air or what?'

I watched them curiously. There was definitely a physical attraction and there was an odd chemistry too, despite the fact they were so opposite. Certainly Nick was just besotted with Vanessa. She said to me once, 'If I told Nick to jump in the river, he would.' But what helped the relationship was Vanessa's hassle with her stepdad.

She'd say, 'My stepdad had another go at me tonight. He says there's no point in me doing A levels if I don't go on to university. But I know the real reason: he wants me out of the house.'

When Vanessa's mum lined up with her stepdad, Vanessa felt abandoned. Obviously I only ever heard her side of it. But all I can say is, I saw Vanessa's stepdad once and didn't like him, he just stood scowling at us. He looked like one of the gangsters you see in old 1960s newsreels. So I wasn't surprised when Vanessa practically moved into Nick's house. I was just amazed at how quickly she took over. Now, whenever I went out with them, Vanessa automatically assumed the front seat (my old seat). Soon even my tapes weren't in the front any more – instead they were replaced by much more girly songs. And she'd say to me, 'I've told Nick he's allowed to go for a boys' night out on Thursday.' I think I was supposed to reply, 'Oh gee, thanks, Vanessa.' I found the whole thing highly amusing. I mean, occasionally, I'd get Nick to do our Carruthers and Monty routine, as it bugged Vanessa because she couldn't join in. But really, I was happy to fade out of the picture. As I said, I saw Nick and me as just having a holiday friendship. But oddly enough, Vanessa was quite keen to keep me on the scene.

I think she liked to talk to me about Nick's family and how strange they were. She'd say to me, 'Nick's family, do they ever sit down and eat together?'

'I don't know, ask them.'

'I'm sure they don't, you know. Nick always eats in his room.'

Then one day at school Vanessa said to me, 'I had a long chat with Sophie last night . . . what do you think of her?'

'She seems OK,' I said, vaguely.

'At first I thought she was a bit weird,' said Vanessa.

Inside I bristled at this. 'She always seemed spaced out,' continued Vanessa, 'and very difficult to get to know. But last night I got talking and actually, she's really nice – quite funny too. I think she's very lonely, though.'

'Why do you think that?'

'Just a feeling I've got,' said Vanessa. 'I mean, it can't be easy starting at a new school in the fifth year. I wouldn't like to do it. Still, she's told me all about Ryan.'

'Who's Ryan?' I asked.

Vanessa looked pleased. She enjoyed knowing things you didn't. Apparently, Ryan was a boy Sophie had spoken to at a party. He was eighteen, worked for a building society and a dazzling future was already being predicted for him.

'A lot of girls liked him,' said Vanessa, 'but Sophie thinks he might be interested in her. She's not sure, though.'

Up to now I'd had a hungry curiosity about Sophie, eager to find out everything I could about her. She intrigued me. But this latest newsflash was a big disappointment. Somehow, I'd imagined Sophie being above such obvious passions.

Vanessa gushed on. 'Ryan's going to be at Sue Hartnell's eighteenth birthday party at Goddards Sports Centre, this Friday.'

'Just about everyone's been invited to that,' I said.

'Well, Sophie wants to go but it's nearly ten miles away and her dad's going to be late home, so she asked Nick if he'd drive her there, but he's got tickets for this basketball match.'

'Oh, what a shame,' I said, without even a pretence of sincerity.

'Sophie offered him the petrol money, too.'

'Ah, well,' I said, 'it was obviously not meant to be. Sophie will not get to dance with the prince from the local building society. Never mind. Perhaps she can take a mortgage out and meet him that way. She could use the petrol money as a down payment . . . how about that?'

'Stop being silly,' said Vanessa. 'We've got to work on Nick.'

'I'll leave that in your capable hands.'

'Oh no, come on, Ben, he looks up to you.'

'What are you talking about?'

'He does. And when I told Sophie I'd get you on our team, she said how nice you were.'

'Just have to tell her the truth then, won't you . . . Oh, all right then, leave it to me. Sophie shall go to the ball, though he sounds a right dork to me.'

That night I told Nick that if he sacrificed watching basketball to help his sister, that would be a noble deed in a dark world.

'What are you talking about, noble deed?' said Nick. 'Anyway, I've already paid for the tickets.'

'That only makes your deed all the nobler,' I said.

'Look, it's you who's into all this Knights of the Round Table stuff, not me,' said Nick.

But later that evening he relented: he would drive Sophie to the party and pick her up later. Then Vanessa decided she, Nick and myself should all go to the party too.

I hadn't a clue why I agreed. I suppose I was curious to see what Sophie's dream man looked like. I already felt competitive with him, as every time I glanced at myself in a mirror there'd be this phantom Brad Pitt look-alike standing beside me. I couldn't get rid of him. I couldn't wipe that smirk off his face either.

On the night of the party . . .

Vanessa had said she wanted 'both her fellas' in suits. So Nick and I were upstairs in his room smartening ourselves up, while we waited for Vanessa to get back from her nan's. Nick couldn't get the knot in his tie right and I was helping him when the doorbell rang. We went to the top of the stairs but Sophie had already answered the door.

It was Vanessa. She and Sophie stood in the hallway, while we stared down at them. Nick started nudging me. Vanessa was wearing a figure-hugging top. I murmured my approval. But it was Sophie I was staring down at. She looked absolutely stunning.

I'd seen her slouching around the house in jeans and what looked like one of her dad's old jumpers. Tonight, well, actually what she had on wasn't that amazing: a white shirt, a black jacket and black trousers. Yet, she just knocked you dead in it.

I looked and looked.

Before, when I'd seen her, she'd always been slightly out of focus. But now, it was as if I'd been given this new high-powered lens which let me see her with amazing clarity. Her eyes, for instance, weren't just green. They were very, very green. Wonderful wide eyes. Yet her face was all in proportion, with her rounded cheekbones and slightly upturned nose. And those pencil-thin eyebrows.

And her mouth. I loved her mouth and the way it curved up at the sides.

Then all at once the lens turned into an X-ray. For a moment, I was right inside Sophie's head. It was over in a flash. But in that single moment I knew her.

She was a friend I'd known all my life. No, it was more than that. And yet, already it was fading fast. It's like that moment just before you wake up when you catch something from your dream. And you reach forward to see more, but already it's gone. You can't hold on to it. But you know you saw something. And what I saw was Sophie and me together. Only it was far off in the future. Maybe years and years away. I rubbed my eyes, the way you do when you've just been staring into a very bright light. My heart was thumping wildly.

Then Vanessa looked up, nudged Sophie and they were both smiling up at us, in our suits. As I tottered down those stairs I felt drunk and dizzy and excited. It was as if I were coming down from the top of a very high mountain, where I had seen something so wonderful, it set me free from all the everyday things.

Then Vanessa made some cracks about the way I'd walked down the stairs. 'You're not drunk already, are you, Ben?'

'I'm merely drunk with ecstasy at the sight of two such bewitching young damsels,' I said.

'Where?' asked Nick.

'All right, calm down, Ben,' said Vanessa. 'He's definitely on something tonight.'

Sophie was smiling her teasing smile at me. I wanted to say, 'Don't waste your time on this Ryan geek. I'm the guy you'll end up with, so come on, give fate a nudge and go away with me tonight.'

I nearly said it, too. I felt reckless.

I smiled at her.

'You look happy,' she said.

'Yes, I am,' I said. One day I'd tell her what I'd seen. And then she'd smile, too. This was a secret I longed to share with her.

'I've never been to an eighteenth or to Goddards, before,' she said suddenly, wide-eyed. 'No one in my year has.'

'So you're the first,' I said, laughing just a little at her, yet admiring her openness too.

'I know it'll be good,' she said. 'It's just I hate the first bit, walking in . . .'

'Being a newcomer,' I interrupted.

'Yes.' She smiled at me.

'It takes time to . . . dissolve into a party,' I said. 'First thing I always do is get a drink. Then I find a spot where I can survey the scene.' She was listening to what I said very carefully, as if I were some kind of expert (which I'm definitely not). It was very flattering.

'Yes, I know I'll enjoy it, once I've got into it,' she said. Then she added, 'Thanks for persuading him.' She nodded at Nick, currently giving Vanessa her I-haven't-seen-you-for-ten-minutes kiss.

' 'Twas nothing,' I said.

'Oh yes it was. Normally my brother wouldn't drive me to the end of the road.'

'You often ask him to drive you to the end of the road, then?'

She laughed. 'Oh, all the time.'

Then Vanessa joined us. 'Getting nervous, Sophie?'

Sophie looked away. 'I'm just going to enjoy myself and see what happens . . .'

'Ryan will be waiting there for us,' interrupted Vanessa. 'You can be sure of that.'

Sophie continued to look away. 'I just want to have a good time, that's all,' she said.

Half an hour later we arrived at Goddards Sports Centre. It was situated in this grey, drab block. And all around it were equally dismal-looking blocks. I said, 'It looks a bit like a prisoner-of-war camp here. We'll probably see someone tunnelling out in a minute.'

'Like that film, *The Great Escape*,' laughed Sophie. All the way there we'd been making silly comments. I felt we were allies. I kept forgetting about Ryan. But Vanessa hadn't. She was getting really high on this matchmaking while my feeling of elation was fading fast. I just didn't want to see Sophie link up with Ryan.

As we got out of the car Vanessa looked at her watch. 'We're late. Ryan will be waiting by the door.'

He wasn't. Sophie laughed nervously. 'I'm really not expecting anything tonight,' she half-chanted.

Vanessa seemed to take his absence as a personal insult. 'He must be here somewhere.' She took Sophie's arm. 'Come on, we'll find him.'

They dived into the party. I joined Nick at the bar. We got our drinks and watched the usual rent-a-crowd around us. Nick kept nudging me, trying to be funny. 'Will you look at that girl. Has she got net curtains over her chest or what?'

But I didn't want to look at her, or anyone, except Sophie. Was she with him yet? Already, I was wishing I hadn't come. Then two guys we knew from the sports centre came over and Nick started waffling on about how he and I should go there more often. I smiled and agreed, and stopped listening.

Was Sophie with him? I had to know.

'I won't be long,' I said to Nick.

He looked surprised, even a bit disappointed. I pushed my way over to the dance-floor area. Lots of people were standing on this grey carpet but hardly anyone was dancing. The carpet had glitter all over it. At the edge of the room were some long tables. One row was made up of couples, the men in their grey trousers and V-necked jumpers, the women with their hair so stiffly permed, it wouldn't move in a tornado. Another table was populated by older women, in their Sunday best. They looked like the ones who grab me at weddings and demand I do the foxtrot with them.

But Sophie wasn't anywhere I could see. Maybe she'd gone outside with him. That thought was like a knife going through me. And then I did spot her – and Vanessa. They were alone.

'We can't see him anywhere,' said Vanessa. I darted a glance at my watch. It was nearly ten o'clock now. He wasn't coming, was he? My heart turned a somersault. I really didn't think there was a chance he'd turn up now. So I could afford to be positive. 'There's time yet, he'll be here.'

'You think so?' said Vanessa.

'He might be really bricking it,' I said. 'He's only got your word that Sophie's interested in him. He could still be turned down, and men's egos are more fragile than you think. He's probably psyching himself up somewhere.'

My insincere drivel actually reassured them. Nick came over. A slow dance was being played and, for the first time, the floor was full of couples. Nick and Vanessa joined the throng. I stood watching them with Sophie. There was a slightly awkward silence between us. I sensed Sophie felt ill at ease, a bit lost. I wasn't quite sure what to say to her.

'You needn't stay with me,' began Sophie. 'I mean, I'm all right.' She was biting her upper lip. One of her little gestures that I'd noticed.

'Actually, I could do with a drink. How about you, Sophie?'

'Oh, yes, thanks.'

We forced our way to the front of the bar. 'What would you like, Sophie?'

Sophie stared around her. 'It's difficult to choose, isn't it?' She looked like a little girl in a sweet shop. Then she turned to me. 'What would you recommend?'

'I don't know, girls always like yukky drinks, like Bacardi and blackcurrant.'

'That's what I'll have,' she said, at once.

When I handed her the drink she sniffed it for a moment, then took a sip. 'Mmm, it's nice. I like it. Actually, I've never had it before.'

She took another sip, holding the glass with both hands, as if it were a cup of tea. I loved her inexperience and the way she tried to carry things off. I wanted to say, 'You're doing really well,' but I was afraid that would sound patronising so I grinned at her. She smiled back but then I saw her eyes slide away from me and over to the entrance. I wanted so badly to keep her attention. All her attention. So I found myself saying, 'This party needs livening up. Now if I were here with my friends Simon and Jenny, I know what we'd do: we'd set each other dares.'

'Dares?'

'Yeah, we'd get each other to do really stupid things.'

'Like what?'

'Anything. Go on then, give me a dare. What are you

laughing at?' I said, mock-indignant. 'Dares are a serious business.'

'Oh, I'm so sorry.' She was still giggling. Her eyes caught mine. We held the look for a moment.

'All right, I want you to . . .' She pointed to the orange curtains at the back of the room. 'I want you to pull back the curtains on both those windows.'

'Easy,' I laughed. But it was then, with immaculate timing, the bouncer lumbered into view. He wasn't big; he was outrageously big. His head was the size of a car.

'Look at him,' gasped Sophie. 'He's like a monster.' Then she looked at me. 'I think we'd better forget about the dare.'

I hesitated. But then I drew myself up. 'My lady has set me a task and I must perform it.'

She put her hand on my arm. 'No, Ben . . .'

But my heart was racing now. 'Farewell,' I said, 'and if I don't return, keep this in memory of me.' I dug around in my pocket and whipped out a blue handkerchief. 'It's pretty clean, I think, and every time you blow your nose, remember me.'

She took it, and half-waved it at me. Then she smiled and whispered, 'Hurry back.'

I just tore across that dance floor, then picked my way around the tables. One woman, who was moaning about the loudness of the music, watched me curiously. And then I came face to face with the orange curtains. For a moment I just pawed at them. I was thinking of that bouncer. Then I pictured Sophie watching me and with one mighty stroke I pulled the first curtain right back. Dazzling blue-green floodlights poured into the room. I turned round triumphantly, ignoring the puzzled looks and angry mutterings around me.

Sophie was waving my blue handkerchief at me. She was really getting into the spirit of this, now. She was brilliant. I bowed, but I knew my task wasn't complete. There was still one more window to liberate. I reached out, gave the curtain a quick tug and now all the windows were ablaze with light. I surveyed my handiwork proudly, until I felt a heavy hand on my shoulder. I slowly turned around, then gasped. For a girl, she had a remarkably strong grip. But who was she and why was she smiling at me? Then I remembered. She was Sue Hartnell; this was her birthday party!

'Hi, Ben,' she said. 'Are you having a good time?'

I was very embarrassed. 'Yes, great, excellent. Oh, and happy birthday.'

'Thanks, Ben. Have you met my mum?' The woman who'd been moaning about the loudness of the music gingerly extended one hand. Then after I'd made a very swift exit, I heard her whisper, 'He just came up here and pulled all the curtains back.'

I started to laugh. And Sophie would laugh when I told her. Only, where was she? Walking off while I'm performing a daring deed *for her*. That's strictly against the rules.

Then I heard my name being called. And there was Vanessa, gazing down at the bunch of roses in her arms.

'Ben, aren't they lovely,' she gushed.

'They surely are,' I said. So Nick had arranged for Vanessa to receive flowers here. I was amazed at my protégé.

Vanessa smiled dreamily. 'And he's sent seven red and five white to show he's starting to fall in love.'

I liked that, the red rose of passion beginning to overtake the white.

'That's why he was so late,' said Vanessa. 'To get those roses he had to go all the way over to . . .'

I suddenly realised we were talking about Ryan. Then I saw him walking over from the bar with Sophie and Nick. He was laughing, Sophie was laughing. Even Nick – whom I'd never seen so much as smile within a two-mile radius of his sister before – was grinning his head off.

And all thanks to Ryan. RYAN.

He was tall (almost my height) and quite well built, with straight hair pushed all the way back. He also wore a T-shirt that was two sizes too small for him, so he could show off his bit of muscle.

I suppose he was good-looking in a goofy way. He was definitely a bit of a lad, but a lad with pretensions. Someone who thought he knew how to socialise with people. When he was introduced to me, he stretched out his hand, saying, 'I've heard all about you, Ben. It's good to meet you,' and gave his 'sincere' smile, a seducer's smile, the smile of someone who's used to getting his own way.

'I hear you're in a drama group, Ben,' he continued, conversationally. No doubt he'd been taught to do that at his building society: find out what your client's interested in and flatter him by asking questions about it. But I was up to all his tricks; his oily charm didn't fool me though I let him think it did. Already I'd sussed out his big weakness: he overrated himself. But what was he really: half-man, half-pin-up. He was nothing. And he was completely wrong for Sophie.

At the moment she seemed overwhelmed by him. And who could blame her? All this fuss and hype and those wretched roses. Ryan was saying, 'I couldn't take my eyes off Sophie but I never thought I had a chance.'

And she was just lapping it up. But soon she'd see through him and realise just how contrived he actually was. But it was so hard, watching all this, twisting my face into smiles. It was almost a relief when Ryan saw some of his friends and took Sophie away: his new trophy.

'They go well together, don't they?' said Vanessa. She

seemed enchanted by them and her role in all this. She even declared, 'If it hadn't been for Ben and me they might never have got together tonight.'

Nick remained unimpressed. 'Those flowers must have cost him a bomb,' was his only comment.

Vanessa turned to me. 'We did it, didn't we?'

'Yes, we did it,' I murmured. But I couldn't contort my face into any more smiles, so instead, I mumbled something about needing another drink.

Across the room the curtains were drawn again. It was as if my dare had never happened. I had a sudden mad urge to go and pull them back again, just for my own pleasure this time. But instead, I submerged myself in a couple of drinks and then I got talking to this girl I'd never seen before. She was called Helen and she told me her hands were freezing and asked if I'd warm them up. She must have held on to my hands for about five minutes.

I'd just finished my impression of a radiator and was chatting to her and being vaguely funny – I was laughing away – when I felt something bubbling in my nose. Then I felt something warm on my hand. The first few drops of blood had landed. Luckily the lights were off and it was really dark, so Helen didn't see anything. I sprang up, mumbled to her that I had to go, then sped off. I get these sudden nosebleeds. But never one like this before.

Of course I didn't have my handkerchief. I shoved a bit of tissue up my nose and joined this massive queue for the loos.

I was terrified someone I knew would spot me as the last thing I wanted was a big scene, with everyone saying, 'Are you all right?' and 'What's happened to you, ha ha?' So I kept my hand over my face, while blood continued to gush out. What if I couldn't stop it? I started to panic. As I walked into the loo the bright lights assaulted me and I was acutely conscious that I was covered in blood. I stumbled about, unable to get anywhere near the mirror. But at last it was stopping. Finally, it stopped, and I decided to escape outside and take a few deep breaths. But on my way out someone called my name.

It was Sophie.

I looked around me. There was a slow dance and the floor was full of couples. But Sophie seemed to be on her own.

She rushed over, then she smiled rather shyly at me. 'Hello.'

'Hello,' I said, grateful that it was dark and she couldn't see my face.

'Everything's just happened so fast,' she said, 'and I can't take it all in, but I . . .' her smile broadened, 'I never told you how great you were, the way you just pulled the curtains back. It was wonderful. And all those people were looking at you, but you, you just went right on . . .'

I thought she'd forgotten. When all the time she was just waiting for the right moment to congratulate me.

'I'm glad you liked it,' I replied, rather lamely. But my head was in the clouds.

'Anyway, let me give you your handkerchief back.' Sophie started digging into her pocket. 'You certainly deserve it.'

And at the moment it would have come in pretty useful. But I said, 'No, don't give it back, keep it.'

'Are you sure?' And she sounded as if I were giving her something really valuable.

'Just remember, Sophie, every time you blow your nose, think of me.'

She giggled. Then she stretched out her hand to me. I think she meant me to kiss it. I leant forward, but then the lights started coming up. Immediately I backed off. It was too late.

'Ben . . . your face,' she gasped.

'Yeah, it's all right, never fear, I haven't been attacked by a monster or anything, just had a massive nosebleed. I'm always getting them. Lucky me, bye.' I fled to the loos again and this time I barged my way through to the mirror. When I saw myself I nearly wept. I looked as if I'd been blooded in a hunt. Then I noticed I had blood all over my white shirt, too. I'd really let myself down tonight.

When I came out Sophie had those flowers in her hand and she was standing with Ryan, Nick and Vanessa.

I actually carried off this part of the evening quite well, walking over to them with a bit of a swagger and tossing aside any expressions of concern. But inside, I was dead. And as I sat squashed in the back of Nick's car with Sophie, Ryan and those wretched roses, I thought bitterly of what I'd seen at the top of the stairs, my little vision of the future. Only it hadn't been a vision at all. No, it was just my imagination stretching out to see what it wanted to see. It was a mirage. A fake. I started to laugh at myself: sad, mocking laughter. Now all I wanted was to crawl into my bedroom, close the door tightly and be on my own. I also made a vow that I'd never put myself in this situation again. What was the point? I'd lost. Nick didn't need me any more, he had Vanessa now. So I really could fade out of that friendship. It was all over.

Nick dropped me home first. And I decided to exit with some style. So as I opened the car door, I said to Sophie and Ryan, 'Don't forget to invite me to the wedding, then.' Everyone was still cackling at that as Nick drove away. I stood staring after the car. Then slowly I walked inside. I really thought I'd never see Sophie again.

7 . . . Knight in Exile

Next day I put myself down for extra hours at the video shop. As Simon commented, I was practically living in there. Simon and Jenny still looked in, other times Nick and Vanessa appeared, bringing news of Sophie. To my deep regret, the news was always good. Vanessa said she'd never seen Sophie 'look so happy'.

I was just getting more and more lost. Until in the end, I decided I enjoyed being lost. If I'd been banished from the 'Kingdom of Couples', then so be it: I would live happily and triumphantly in exile. So though Nick talked about 'boys' nights out' and doing more events at the sports centre, I never picked up on his suggestions. Instead, every night after I closed up the video shop I went for a walk, alone.

Soon it became a ritual. And somehow, I always ended up sitting right beside the tree at the top of Windmill Hill. It was a good spot as I could see everything for miles around. I could even make out Sophie and Nick's house. I'd picture them: Nick trying to watch the football, Vanessa flapping about, organising everyone; their parents scuttling around, then Sophie coming in with Ryan, who'd be all oily and smiley . . . I saw it all. But up here it didn't matter. Up here I could smile down on their little lives. For now I was raised above them; I was all powerful.

Then I'd return home and even though it was late and my family had long since gone to sleep and my bedroom was full of heavy darkness, I wouldn't be at all tired. So I'd put the TV on low in my room. Channel 4 was running a season of very old, black and white Cary Grant films.

I'd lie on my bed and watch all these long-dead people moving and smiling and kissing. Sometimes I'd look them up in my film book. When their face was held in close-up and they'd stare through the screen at me, I'd whisper: 'I know your whole life; how many films you'll make, who you'll marry, when you'll die,' and it was just as if I were on top of Windmill Hill again. All these people in my room lay deep in the earth somewhere. They didn't exist any more. They were just shadows now. And yet, they were more real than anyone I knew, especially old Cary Grant, in his double-breasted suits with his white shirts and thickly knotted ties.

There was one film of his I especially liked: it was the one where he rescues Ingrid Bergman at the end. She's being poisoned by her husband (who's an enemy agent) and no one realises. No one, except Cary. I love the scene at the end where he sneaks into her bedroom. She hugs him, but she is too weak to walk. So then, he picks her up in his arms and starts carrying her down the stairs. And her husband and all the other enemy agents are at the bottom of the stairs. But Cary just keeps on going. And it's as if he's untouchable, somehow. I could watch that scene over and over. It's brilliant.

I bought a couple of double-breasted suits from Oxfam. I dug out some white shirts and I copied the way Cary did his ties. I even slicked my hair back, like him. I looked pretty slick, actually. But what did I end up doing? Kissing a girl outside the chip shop.

I'd just closed up the video shop when I heard my name being called. It was Helen from the party. She was standing outside the chip shop and she was very drunk. I went over to her and she cried, 'I'm drunk enough to be frank. I really fancy you.' Then she started to kiss me. It seemed rude not to join in. And we were there for ages, until she asked me if I wanted to go back to her house as there was no one in . . . nudge, nudge. I thought this was all a bit too easy so I mumbled something about having to get back. At once, she became really aggressive, demanding to know, 'Are you turning me down because I've had a baby?'

I didn't know she had a baby. I didn't even know her full name. Then she told me she'd just broken up with her boyfriend; her parents had taken the baby for the night and told her to go out and have a good time. I should have guessed she was on the rebound. I'm the rebound king. She rambled on about how unhappy she was and how she was looking for someone just like me. So I walked her home. But that was it. I was sick of rescuing people. Anyway, she'd be back with her boyfriend within a week. I'd bet money on it.

She did make a point of inviting me in again. And I was almost tempted. But it wasn't what I wanted, not like that. So what did I want? It was hard to explain. No it wasn't: I wanted there to be some meaning to it.

Next day at drama Vanessa said to me, 'You were seen kissing a girl last night.'

'Oh no, hold the front page.'

Vanessa gave me a strange smile. 'I guessed there was someone. I told Nick that's why we hadn't seen you much.'

52

It was at that meeting Ernie, our drama teacher, made a major announcement. Ernie had a face that was so red you could see his little nerve endings. He also had a habit of putting his head round the door and just staring, which could be very eerie. And when he was angry, he would suddenly yell across the room at you. Most people thought he was weird but no one messed with him. I rather liked him. Once I went to see him in a play at the town hall; he only had a small role – as this vicar who discovers he's an atheist – but he was pretty good.

That afternoon he was in his Tintin T-shirt – he always did that to stress how informal the group was – and was talking excitedly about a new competition.

'All you've got to do,' he said, 'is write a play lasting for twenty minutes, involving not more than four characters. These have to be submitted by 20 December, that's just three weeks away. But then, if your play is picked as one of the seven best, the group will be invited to put it on at a special drama competition.' He paused expectantly. I was mildly interested, but that was all.

Someone asked, 'Does the winner get any money?'

Ernie looked pained. 'There *is* a cash prize.'

'How much?' asked several voices now.

'Four hundred pounds.' There were loud cheers. 'And eight hundred pounds to the school.' There were equally loud boos. Ernie raised his head, his white hair making a brilliant contrast to his bright red face. 'This is an important competition – and we should certainly enter. I'll help all I can. But first, we need someone to write the play.' Suddenly, he was looking at me. The whole group were. 'Ben, do you think you can write a play for us – first draft by next week?'

'Next week,' I echoed.

'Yes, I wanted to give you a bit of time,' he said. That was his little joke. 'Come on, Ben, this could be your chance.'

I made protesting noises but the idea was taking hold. That night I tried out some ideas. And the next. And the next . . . soon I adopted a nightly ritual. I'd begin by reading and then tearing up last night's ideas. Then I'd attempt another idea which would be torn up the following night. And so it went on.

At the next drama meeting I told Ernie I'd had a go but none of my ideas were any good. 'Keep trying,' he said. And then, that night, almost out of nowhere . . . I was watching another Cary Grant film, the last in the season and not one of his best. But it still fascinated me, especially the close-ups, when these gleaming dead faces would float towards me. And suddenly, I wondered what it must be like if once you'd known one of those shadows. Once you'd loved a girl with dark hair, big wide eyes and a little gap between her two front teeth.

Without my even realising it, the girl was turning into Sophie. Only her hair was blonde, not dark like Sophie's. What if it were Sophie? Years ago, I'd loved her and lost her – I wasn't sure how, yet – and now she was dead and I was an old, old man. But at night her eyes still flicked towards me, young, beautiful, alive. She was there in her kingdom of black and white, while I was imprisoned here, gazing at her through the bars of real life. I could never reach her. Or could I?

I sat up all night writing that first draft. There were four characters: an old man, his granddaughter, her fiancé and the character I'd called 'Sophie'. The main character had been a famous writer, but now he was old, and lonely and hardly ever saw his daughter. In fact, he hardly saw anyone. And then Katie, his granddaughter, came to call with her fiancé, Alex; that was how the play opened. At first the grandfather was cold to them but then he saw just how much they were in love. And late at night, he put on a video of an old film, for which he'd written the script. It was the last scene. The girl who was acting in it was beautiful. She was alone on the screen. Her lover was dead and her family had told her to forget him: 'Forgetting him would be like forgetting myself.' Then she said softly, to her dead lover, 'I'll be waiting . . . I'll wait for you for ever.' The scene ends with her walking off into the distance, alone. The grandfather told them the actress was called 'Sophie', and she was the only girl he had ever loved but, through a tragic misunderstanding, he'd lost her and now she was dead. He urged them to marry at once.

Katie began to feel sorry for her grandfather and one evening, a few days later, she and Alex visited again. The front door was open, and inside the video was playing the same scene from the film they'd watched that night. But where was her grandfather? Alex looked upstairs. And then Katie stared at the screen in amazement. For this time, 'Sophie' was not walking into the distance alone: someone was walking beside her. It was her grandfather, only looking years younger. He saw Katie and waved; so did 'Sophie'. Then 'Sophie' reached out her hand to him and they walked away, just as Alex called. He'd found her grandfather upstairs; he must have had a heart attack, he was dead. The play ended with Katie whispering, 'But he's not dead, he's just started to live.'

Maybe it sounds a bit corny. But I didn't want it to be corny. That's why I wrote and rewrote those opening scenes that night. What really fired me was the idea of seeing someone you loved so much just centimetres away from you, while at the same time knowing they were as far away from you as it was possible to be. Photographs were bad enough. I remember when my grandad died,

Nan locked away all the photo albums. 'It brings back too much,' she said. But to see the person you loved talking and moving about, to see all their little gestures . . . that could tear you apart. I suppose my ending was pure fantasy. You can never go back. Time is ruthless, and all powerful – except in my play.

Next day I could hardly keep my eyes open at school. So I came home at lunchtime and went straight to sleep. And then I started dreaming about Sophie. And when I woke up it was as if she was still in the room. My head was flooded with pictures of her: first I was looking down the stairs at her, then she was smiling at me, saying, 'I never told you how brilliant you were,' and there she was, gazing at me out of a black and white film. Only that wasn't Sophie at all. Not the real Sophie. Or was it? Somehow, all my pictures of Sophie were running into each other. I felt as if I were still dreaming. Then the doorbell rang.

I quickly got dressed and rushed downstairs. I opened the door to see Jenny standing there. I gazed at her in amazement.

She grinned at me. 'You've been a long time. Hoping I'd go away, were you?'

'How did you know?'

It was quite a shock seeing her on my doorstep. It had been months since she'd called round.

'Put the kettle on, then, Ben, I'm gasping,' demanded Jenny, marching into the kitchen just as she used to. I looked at her. The giant earrings she always wore. Her big boots. Those chains. Everything about Jenny is over the top, but especially her hair. She's got this mane of red hair and it's awesome. It's like one of those wigs from Charles II's time. On anyone else it would seem ludicrous. But with Jenny, any other style wouldn't work. Jenny with short hair is unimaginable. She hovered around me, while I made her coffee and toast. And we resumed the bantering tone we always adopted with each other.

'So why aren't you working away in your cake shop? Skiving, are you?' I asked.

'No,' she said, indignantly. Then she smiled, 'Well, in a way. It's only, this morning I didn't feel too well and I thought I'd better not go in, in case I've got anything infectious.'

'You're just so caring.'

'I know. But actually, I feel much better now. So I thought, who shall I go and see?'

'And you worked your way down to me.'

'Yeah, you were the last name on my list. I saw your mum and dad out in the car yesterday with Glen. They all waved.'

'That must have been the highlight of your day.'

'Glen was all dressed up. Was he going to a party?'

'Probably. He's always going to parties. Terrible really, six years old and already he's getting invited to more parties than me.'

'He looked so cute.'

'Not as cute as me.'

'No one's as cute as you, Ben,' she said, her eyes flashing with laughter. 'I haven't spoken to your mum and dad for ages. Or Glen.' She paused for just a moment. 'Or you.'

'What are you rabbiting on about,' I said. My heart was thumping fast and I had a feeling Jenny's was too. I started busying myself around the kitchen, hardly knowing what I was doing. 'I'm always seeing you,' I said.

'Oh, we see you in the video shop, but that's just a little snippet, that's nothing, really.' She got up. 'I feel bad about . . .'

'About what?' I snapped. I wasn't being exactly helpful. I was too worked up.

'Look, are you making those coffees or not?'

'You're so impatient.'

'I've been here about twenty minutes.'

'Ah, but this coffee is worth waiting for . . . and you've been here for exactly seven and a half minutes. It just feels like twenty.'

She grinned at me. 'That must be it.' We went into

the lounge. At once, Jenny started peering at me as if I were some difficult mathematical problem she was trying to solve.

'What?' I demanded rudely.

'You've really got the hump with me . . . us.'

'What are you talking about?'

'No, you have, and I don't blame you. It all happened so fast. I mean, I honestly thought Simon and I were just mates, very special mates – like you and me.' She stared at me expectantly.

'Shut up and drink your coffee.'

'You can be so annoying,' said Jenny.

'Me?'

'Yes, you,' she cried. 'You're getting me so mad. I mean, I'm trying to explain it to you, and apologise.'

'Go on then,' I said.

She sighed, dramatically. 'What I'm saying is, none of this was expected. I didn't even know Simon liked me in that way. And then everything just felt so muddled. And I wanted to play things down, take it slowly. I mean, the number of girls who meet some bloke and go on and on about how much they like him. I've done it myself. And then you get this big smack in the teeth when it doesn't work out. That's why, this time, I thought, I'll just take things as they come. And I didn't want to talk about it to anyone . . . not even you. Not until I knew . . .'

'Knew what?' I asked, unhelpfully.

'Knew if Spurs were going to be relegated this season. What do you think?'

'OK, I get it. So now you know.'

'I think so,' she said softly. 'With Simon it's so difficult. He never gives much away, does he? Even about his mum, do you remember?'

'I remember,' I said.

Shortly before I knew him, Simon's mum had walked out on him, his younger brother and his dad. He never saw her or heard from her for ages. Then one day when Jenny and I were away on a field trip his mum turned up at the school, right out of the blue, wanting to see him. But Simon never even mentioned it to us. When we found out and confronted him, Simon just said, 'There was nothing to tell you. She turned up, tried to talk to me and I just walked away from her. She'd left it too late. We don't need her any more.' He never mentioned the incident again.

Jenny continued, 'I'd keep asking myself, does he really care about me or not? So one Sunday morning I went round his house and said, "I think we need to go for a walk." We took his dog out and wandered round this field and then I told him I thought we should finish. I didn't want to finish at all, really. I just wanted to see how he reacted, if it mattered . . .'

'And did he pass the test?' I asked, drily.

Jenny laughed nervously. 'As soon as I said it his face just crumpled. He was so concerned and anxious. And we spent all day together, talking. And Simon's dad knew something was wrong and he kept saying to Simon in the kitchen, "You don't want to lose her, she's special."'

'I bet you revelled in all this.'

'I felt terrible, actually. As if I didn't deserve Simon, putting him through all that. But it wasn't just a silly game. I had to see if he really cared before I committed myself, I suppose. I don't know ... anyway, now it's good, really good.' She stopped and looked at me expectantly. I knew what that look meant. So far she'd made all the effort: coming here, apologising, explaining. Now it was my turn.

So what could I say? Tell her how badly I felt when she started going out with Simon. But what was the point of bringing all that up? She and Simon were a couple. End of story. And if I couldn't accept that then I wasn't really much of a friend. I'll be your friend but only if you do what I want. What use was that to anyone? It was tough, though. I still felt they'd left me out. And part of me wanted to go away and nurse my grievance. Yet, I also knew if I didn't take this chance to repair things, there might not be another.

'When you and Simon went out together I was pretty shocked,' I began, 'especially as . . . well, you do have a knack for picking the wrong guy.'

'Tell me about it,' began Jenny.

'But this time . . . this time you haven't picked the wrong guy.'

Without another word Jenny got up and gave me a hug.

'I have missed you,' she whispered.

'I've missed you too,' I said.

'Are you doing anything tonight?' she asked.

'I don't think so.'

'You are now.'

'Am I allowed to know what?'

'You're taking me out for a drink – don't forget.'

'I won't,' I said.

But I never saw Jenny that night. Mum was just serving dinner when the phone rang. I answered it and, to my surprise, it was Vanessa. She'd only rung me once before – the night after her first date with Nick.

'Hi, Ben, how are you?' but she rushed on before I could answer. 'I'm sorry to bother you, but something awful's happened. Sophie's cut her wrists.'

6 . . . Rescuing Sophie

Vanessa opened the door. 'Thanks for coming round, Ben. I knew you would.'

We went into the lounge. 'How is she?' I asked.

'All right, now,' she said, slowly.

'So what exactly happened?'

'Ten days ago Ryan finished with Sophie. He was waiting for her after school, told her he wanted to end it and then just walked off. It was a total shock. But she took it really well, even joked about it, saying that she'd heard he never went out with a girl for longer than a month and she'd made six weeks . . . I really admired the way that she seemed to accept it.

'And then after school I couldn't face going home and Nick was at weight-training, so I borrowed his key and then I . . . I heard Sophie in her bedroom. I went upstairs . . . she'd cut her wrists. I was in such a panic. How I found her mum's work number I don't know. We were helping, weren't we, Ben?' She looked so lost, that I took her hand. She held on to it.

'They haven't said anything, but I'm sure the family blame me.'

'If anyone's to blame, it's me,' I replied. 'I'm the one who persuaded Nick to drive Sophie to that party.'

'Thanks . . . thanks.' She slowly let go of my hand.

Nick appeared. He grinned and clapped me on the back. 'If it isn't Carruthers. Where have you sprung from?'

Vanessa answered. 'I told Ben about Sophie cutting her wrists.'

The smile left Nick's face. He immediately turned away. 'Only scratched her wrists . . .' he muttered. Then he turned round. 'People split up all the time. Anyway, she's only known him five minutes. So what's she making all this fuss about.' He sounded indignant and scared.

'There are ways of breaking up with people,' said Vanessa. 'He did it very brutally. You should feel sorry for your sister.'

'Don't tell me what I should feel,' cried Nick. 'I'm off out.'

'Where are you going?' demanded Vanessa at once.

'Just out.' But then he added, 'I'll be at the Red Lion with my mates, if anyone's interested.'

After he'd gone Vanessa declared, 'This family's so weird. When their dad came home he just went upstairs, saw Sophie for about a minute, that's all, then legged it to the greenhouse.'

And probably if Sophie had killed herself he'd still be in that greenhouse, pruning a wreath or something. I felt protective towards her.

'You'll see her, won't you?'

'Yeah, sure, if it's OK with Sophie.'

'Oh, yes, she knows I rang you. She wants to see you.'

I sprinted up those stairs. Sophie's mum was hovering rather uncertainly outside Sophie's room. 'I've just been in,' she said, smiling faintly at me. 'Luckily it wasn't a deep cut, so there was no need to call the doctor, but it gave us a scare . . . She doesn't believe in herself, that's her trouble.' Sophie's mum hesitated, as if she was about to say something else. But in the end she just asked, 'Would you like a cup of tea? I'm making one.'

'Yes, thanks,' Vanessa and I chorused, more out of awkwardness than anything else.

'And I've got some Battenberg cake too,' she said.

I'd have agreed to eat anything. I just wanted to see Sophie.

Sophie's mum made as if to go, then turned round

and said, with surprising force, 'That boy should be punished for what he's done. Well he won't be setting foot in here again.'

Her bedroom was tiny. There was barely space for her bed. There were a few rather arty postcards on the wall and just one very old black and white photograph, of a woman, standing with her arms folded and smiling rather apprehensively. Sophie was sitting on top of her bed, in a light blue nightie, playing a computer game. And she was staring at it intently, as if nothing else mattered.

Then, suddenly she looked up, saw me and whispered, 'It's Sir Lancelot.' And she said it almost as a joke, yet very affectionately, too. Our private joke. I don't think Vanessa heard her. Those words were meant just for me.

Vanessa asked Sophie how she was.

'I'm OK . . . I don't know.' She shrugged her shoulders in a sad, defeated gesture, as if she had no energy left. Then I saw the plasters on her wrists and immediately felt a surge of anger. How I wanted to make Ryan see what he'd done. But he couldn't see it, even if he were here. Only I could see the pain burning inside Sophie. Sophie looked at me and gave a wry smile. 'I was a bit silly today.'

'He's just not worth it,' said Vanessa.

'No, I know that.'

'You gave us such a scare,' said Vanessa, sounding like a concerned teacher. 'Why did you do it?'

'I don't know.' She gave another wry smile. 'It was just I . . .' She raised her hand as if to stop the words slipping away. 'I saw all this emptiness and I didn't know how to fill it.'

'Well, next time you feel that just ring me,' said Vanessa. 'If you talk about things you always feel much better, don't you, Ben?'

'That's true,' I murmured. I was watching Sophie with a sharp, stabbing sympathy, yet a strange excitement too. Suddenly, I could see a role for myself. If only Vanessa would leave, then I could hug Sophie and tell her, 'I'm here now. Everything's fine.' And then I could take her in my arms and carry her out of the house, just as Cary Grant had done with Ingrid Bergman in that film.

But instead Sophie's mum returned with tea and Battenberg for all. Sophie hardly spoke and she looked so pale and washed out. Nick might say she'd only known Ryan for five minutes but what mattered was not how long but what you felt and how much you felt. I didn't want to leave Sophie, but I couldn't reach her with her mum and Vanessa thronging about.

Next day I rang up to find out how Sophie was.

'She's better – I think,' said her mum.

She said the same thing when I rang the following

day. I knew I could help Sophie but not at her house.

And then one Saturday I saw her in town. I'd been working in the video shop and I was on my lunch break. Ernie thought watching a play might help me with my own so I went to buy three tickets for *Murder by Mistake* as Jenny and Simon wanted to go too. I saw Sophie, walking past the fountain. I called out, but she didn't hear me. She seemed to be in a dream so I half-ran over to her. It was a bitterly cold December day, the wind was like a knife cutting through you. I had on a thick jacket, but Sophie was just wearing a skimpy white top.

'You must be absolutely freezing,' I said.

She seemed to see me for the first time and managed a small smile. Her face was totally drained of colour. I wanted to help her so badly but I wasn't sure what to say. In the end I started peeking into her bag, just for something to do. 'What have you been buying then?'

'Some clothes . . . I've spent all my money.'

I picked up a yellow top. 'This looks like it's just shrunk in the wash.'

'It's supposed to be like that.' She gave me another small smile.

'If you say so . . . where are you off to then?'

'I'm going home actually. Ryan's coming round.'

'Ryan!'

'I've got some of his CDs. He asked me if he could come and collect them.'

'And you said he could?'

She shrugged her shoulders: 'I must have done, they're his CDs . . . My mum says I should throw all his stuff into the road. Would you do that?' she asked.

Too right, I would. I'd throw Ryan's CDs into the road with the greatest of pleasure. And yet I sensed Sophie didn't want me to say that.

'No, I definitely wouldn't. You might feel better for a few minutes but once you make that sort of gesture, well, you can never come back from it, can you? If you meet in the street you'll never even say hello. You'll totally ignore each other as if you'd never met, as if you've wiped that person from your memory bank. You haven't, of course, but you'll have to pretend you have, even to yourself . . . and there's nothing sadder in the world than that.'

'So what would you do?' she asked, quietly.

'I'd answer the door to him, help him get all his things, that'll make him feel far worse, actually, but it also means you're in control, and well, you'll still be talking. You won't be enemies.'

'You're the first one to put it that way.' Her tone was admiring. And in that moment I felt as if we'd turned another corner somehow. For the first time I wasn't just

Nick's friend who was nice to her. I sensed her looking and looking at me. 'So what have you been up to, Ben?'

'This and that. I'm writing a play for the drama group.'

'Really. You do interesting things, don't you? I mean, so many people just go down the pub and get in fights and all that stuff, but you see things differently. I've hardly seen any plays, but I'd like to see some – and I'd love to read yours.'

'OK,' I said. 'You'll be the first to read it.'

'Honestly?' Her eyes lit up for a moment.

'And I'm just getting tickets for *Murder by Mistake*. I'm going with Jenny and Simon. I can get you a ticket too, if you like.' I just blurted that last sentence out. No wonder Sophie looked surprised.

'I'm afraid I've got a bit of a cash-flow problem.'

'I can lend you the money. That's no problem.'

'No. I couldn't do that,' she said.

'Don't be silly,' I replied. 'You're talking to the man who's the very heartbeat of Cartford's video store. I've saved a small fortune. I'm practically a millionaire.'

She started to smile. 'So, what night?'

'Wednesday.'

'Well, I don't think I'm doing anything. Could I ring you?'

'Yeah, sure, have you got my number?'

'Nick will have it.'

'Of course he will.' I felt suddenly embarrassed. I'd pushed too hard. 'Well, anyway, I'd better go.'

'Yeah, so had I. Thanks for your advice.'

'Giving advice is nothing,' I said.

'I don't think so.'

I hesitated. I couldn't just leave her looking so vulnerable – and cold. I whipped my jacket off and said, 'Here, borrow this.'

'No, it's all right.'

'Go on,' I said, firmly. 'You'll get pneumonia going round like that.'

It was far too big for her, but that made her look even more appealing. 'I'll get Nick to bring it back.'

'Whatever.' We stood staring at each other.

'See you then, Sir Lancelot,' she said.

Later I went over to the Richardson theatre, and bought four tickets. Then I waited impatiently for Sophie to ring. Every time the phone went I sprang to answer it. But she didn't call until Tuesday night.

'Hi, Ben.' It was the first time she'd ever rung me. And that tremor in her voice sounded louder on the phone. 'Are you still going to the play?' she asked.

'Yeah, are you coming with us?'

'I'm still a bit short of cash.'

'No problem. I've got a spare ticket and it's yours.'

'I will pay you back just as soon as I . . .'

'We'll sort that out later,' I interrupted. 'We're probably going by taxi, so we can pick you up.'

'No, Dad said he'll take me. What time are you getting there?'

'Oh, about half-seven.'

'OK, see you soon, Ben. Bye.'

I put the phone down. I felt energised, flooded with life.

The following afternoon I arranged to meet Simon in town for the first time in ages.

I'd missed him. Simon is quite small and wiry with a long, thin face which doesn't quite match his body. And he's practically impossible to dislike: easy-going, friendly, humorous and not at all pushy.

I don't think I've ever got mad with Simon in my life. Yet, I nearly did that afternoon.

As we roamed around the shops I told him that Sophie would be joining us at the theatre tonight. He was very curious about her and started firing all these questions at me. Then I told him she was fifteen.

'Fifteen.' He started to laugh. 'What are you doing with a fifteen-year-old . . . helping her with her homework, are you?' Simon carried on laughing until he saw my face.

'That's typical of you,' I said. 'I try and tell you something and you stand there making wisecracks.'

Simon immediately backed off. 'I didn't mean anything. I'm sure she's great.'

At once I calmed down. If Simon had told me he was seeing a fifteen-year-old I'd have teased him. So what was I getting so sensitive about?

That night at the theatre Sophie was waiting for us. I can see her now, leaning against the box-office, in my jacket. And I felt a stab of excitement knowing she was waiting there for me. Jenny and Simon couldn't have been friendlier. And although Sophie was clearly shy, she did make an effort to join in the conversation and she tapped into Jenny's humour quickly. The play itself was enjoyably bad. The actors kept making mistakes; at one point one of the actors almost rolled off the stage. Then he got the giggles.

Afterwards, in the bar, Jenny said, 'One day we'll be coming here to see a play by Ben Chaplin.'

Then Sophie said unexpectedly, 'Let's drink a toast to Ben's play – and you'd better invite us all to the first night.'

'Because there won't be a second one,' quipped Simon.

'Shall I kill him for you?' said Jenny.

'If you would,' I replied.

We all solemnly clinked glasses and everyone chanted: 'To Ben's play.' Shortly afterwards Sophie disappeared to the ladies'. 'She's really nice,' said Jenny.

'Very pretty,' said Simon.

'Oi, watch it,' said Jenny. 'No, she is very pretty, got lovely eyes. Did you say she was only fifteen? She seems much older somehow, really sophisticated.'

'Only one thing's bothering me,' said Simon. 'I couldn't be sure – it's just a guess really – but I think she's nicked your jacket. I'd have thought she just had the same naff taste in jackets as you if it weren't nineteen times too big for her.'

'All right, I'll tell you,' I said. 'Sophie and I swop all our clothes.'

'So what are you wearing of hers – or shouldn't we ask?' laughed Jenny.

'No, come on, why is she wearing your coat? Tell us, because we're very nosy.'

'I know that. OK. I saw her in town last Saturday when it was really cold and she was just wearing this silly top . . .' I stopped. Simon and Jenny were both grinning at me.

'And so you gave her your coat,' cried Jenny. 'Oh, Ben, you're just my hero.'

'Yeah, all right,' I muttered.

'We wondered whose white horse that was outside,

didn't we?' said Jenny. 'I can see Ben now, riding through the town centre on his white charger, searching for any young damsels who need rescuing . . .'

'You could be next,' I interrupted.

'Oh, not me,' laughed Jenny. 'I'm what's-her-name, Boadicea. No one rescues me.'

'They wouldn't be able to get you up on the horse,' I said.

'Here, watch it,' grinned Jenny. 'So what is Sophie then, just a friend, or what?'

I sensed they were both watching me intently now. I hesitated. 'She's going through a bad time at the moment. Her boyfriend dumped her and she took it very badly. In fact, the other day she cut her wrists.'

'Oh, no,' cried Jenny.

Immediately I wondered if I should have told them. This was private information, really. And if Sophie found out she'd think I'd been gossiping about her. But that wasn't my intention at all; I just wanted to get Simon and Jenny on her side.

'Don't tell Sophie I told you,' I began.

'Oh yeah, I'm really going to go up to her and say, "I hear you cut your wrists recently," ' cried Jenny. Her tone softened. 'Still, she's coming through it and fair play to her and you. She deserves a bit of help. And if ever she wants to come round my house . . . I mean, you'd better warn her what it's like, a total madhouse, but if ever she wants to . . .'

'I'm sure she would,' I interrupted. 'You ask her.'

And when Sophie returned, Jenny did invite her around and a date was fixed. 'I suppose we'll have to invite you too,' said Jenny to me.

'And I suppose I'll have to accept,' I said. But inside, I felt such a rush of excitement. Another evening with Sophie.

We had just enough money for a taxi home – I slipped Sophie a fiver for her share – and on the way to the taxi rank Sophie said to me, 'I followed your advice about Ryan.'

'You did?'

'When he came round for his things we chatted for quite a while and it was all right, and then just before I came out he rang me. He wanted to see me tonight. But I told him I was going out with you. He said to say hello.'

'Oh yeah,' I said, absently.

'And I'm seeing him tomorrow night, just as friends. He said we should meet up once a week to keep in contact . . . You were the only one who didn't see Ryan as some kind of monster, you know, and that really helped, thanks.'

I'll admit that conversation was a bit of a setback. So Ryan was still skulking about, up to no good. I wanted to shout a warning to her. But that wouldn't work. Sophie had woven a dream around him. That was what she was clinging on to. Besides, they say it's dangerous to wake up a sleepwalker. But Sophie would wake up to his true nature soon enough. And when she did, she'd see me standing right beside her.

5 . . . The Dreams Are Calling

The first time I saw Jenny's mum, I thought she was a
vampire. It was nearly two o'clock in the morning when
I spotted her putting out the washing. This was usual
behaviour for Jenny's parents, who frequently stayed up
longer than Jenny. That's why Jenny's house was so
popular. In other houses, late at night, it was take your
shoes off, don't laugh, don't flush the loo, breathe quietly
. . . At Jenny's house, whatever time you arrived there
were always lights on and activity. Occasionally, Jenny's
mum could get a bit funny about the mess – the house
was always in a muddle – but really, she was incredibly
tolerant and good-humoured. So was her dad. He liked
his little joke, though. You'd ring up and ask if Jenny was

there and he'd reply, 'Yes, she is, thanks for asking. Bye,' and put the phone down.

The night I went round with Sophie, Jenny's parents played Monopoly with us for about two hours. I wondered what Sophie made of this and the easy way Jenny's parents wandered in and out. I thought she was enjoying herself. But it was hard to tell, she looked deathly pale.

Then much later, when just the four of us were sprawled out by the sofa, Jenny said, 'Tell me to mind my own business if you like, Sophie, but have you seen your ex-boyfriend at all?'

Sophie, who was lying on the far end of the sofa, let out a sigh. 'He came round this afternoon, actually.'

'Oh yes,' said Jenny.

'He wanted me to know before anyone else found out. He's seeing someone else.'

'He doesn't waste his time, does he,' cried Jenny. 'So who is she? Did he tell you?'

'Yes, she's called Tania, a girl at his work.'

'Oh, that won't last,' began Jenny.

'She's his boss, actually,' said Sophie.

'His boss,' echoed Jenny.

'Yes,' said Sophie. 'It's all supposed to be top secret. No one must know.'

'I'd send them an anonymous note,' murmured Simon.

'How old is she?' asked Jenny.

'Twenty-five,' said Sophie.

'And he's eighteen,' said Jenny.

'That's right.' Sophie's voice was starting to fade out. 'I think he's been interested in her for a while.'

'And what she can do for him,' added Simon.

There was silence for a moment.

'At least he told you,' declared Jenny. 'You've got to give him that.'

'Oh yes, it can't have been easy,' Sophie said, very quietly. 'And if that's what he really wants, I've no right to make him feel bad about it.'

'Well, you're better than me, there,' said Jenny. 'I like people I break up with to be really miserable for years afterwards.'

'So do I,' said Simon, looking at her. 'I hate people living on without me.'

Sophie turned to me. 'You're very quiet, Ben.'

I'd been terrified that Ryan was about to stage a comeback. But what Ryan had done now was write himself out of Sophie's life for ever; he could never come back from this, could he? I longed to point this out, to draw a line under his name now. But I knew that wasn't the way so I stayed in the guise of Ryan's supporter.

'At least he did tell you, so he's obviously still interested,' I said, knowing this would provoke Jenny. And sure enough, she rushed in.

'Or he might just be keeping his options open. And even if he does come back to you, he could still do it again. I mean, I don't know him or anything, but he was willing to dump you for another girl, that's what it's really about. And I'm sorry to be so blunt, but my advice would be to forget him. Full stop.'

'All right, calm down,' said Simon.

'No, I'm sorry, I know I'm probably being a bit out of order saying this to you, Sophie, and he could be a very nice lad, but he could also be using you. Anyway, if he wants you he'll come running back soon enough, but on your terms, not his. You mustn't wait around for him. Get on with your own life.' She paused. 'You didn't mind me saying that, did you?'

'Not at all,' said Sophie. 'When I saw him I told him I'd been to the theatre and that I was coming round here. I think he was quite amazed actually, at how quickly I've . . . No, I'm getting on with my life all right.' She said this both defiantly and desperately. But there was a flatness and weariness to her voice. More than anything else, I wanted to bring her back to life again.

When I was walking back with Sophie, to my surprise, she suddenly asked, 'When am I going to see your play, then?'

Feeling distinctly chuffed that she'd remembered, I

dived into my house and brought out my copy. She waited shyly in the doorway.

'This isn't your only copy, is it?' she asked.

'Yes.'

'Oh, I can't take this, then,' and she made as if to give it back.

'No, I want you to read it now.'

'But what if I lose it?'

I shrugged my shoulders. 'It's probably total rubbish, anyway.'

The next day I'd just got in from school when Sophie rang.

'I've read your play.'

'Already?'

'I read it when I got in last night. And once I started I couldn't stop.'

'What are you on about?'

'No, really, it captivated me.' That seemed such an unusual phrase. 'It captivated me.' I think I'll always remember her saying that: and the pride I felt.

'You're a very talented man,' she said.

'That's true.'

She laughed. 'Modest, too.'

'Have you got any suggestions . . .?'

'Just one or two small things . . . nothing really. You might even think they're a bit stupid.'

'I'd really like to hear them,' I said. 'And I still need a title.' I hesitated for just a second. 'Are you doing anything tonight?'

'Not a thing.'

'You are now,' I said.

I just told my mum, very casually, that Sophie was coming round to help me with the play. But perhaps because I hadn't invited a girl round for ages, there was a real buzz of anticipation. My mum and dad kept asking me questions about her. I told them she was a friend of Jenny's (that part wasn't exactly a lie) and this made them even more enthusiastic as they really liked Jenny. They also assumed Sophie was the same age as Jenny and I let them go on assuming that. I knew they'd ask a lot more questions if they thought she was only fifteen.

Even Glen picked up the excitement. He kept tearing around the house, yelling, 'When Sofa's coming round?' And although he had been sent to bed, as soon as the doorbell rang he tore downstairs again. Sophie won him over instantly and he paid her his highest compliment: he pulled her outside to admire his collection of sticks.

I watched Sophie chatting with my parents. I always hate that first meeting with your girlfriend's parents, as, however nice they are you know they're trying to suss you out. Are you worthy of her? I knew (although they'd deny it) my parents were doing something similar.

Yet, I also sensed they liked her. And afterwards Dad told me he thought Sophie was 'a real stunner', and my mum said, 'Sophie seemed rather a nervous girl but very nice.'

The interrogation over, I took Sophie upstairs to my bedroom. My bedroom is where I live. All my friends come up there. So Jenny, for instance, had been in my bedroom hundreds of times. She was always leaving her earrings behind.

I suppose my bedroom's more like a clubhouse. It's somewhere to mellow out. Only, when Sophie walked in, it turned into a bedroom again. I felt awkward and self-conscious and all churned up. She sat right on the edge of my bed, with her knees together as if she was wearing a dress, not jeans. And she kept brushing her hair away from her face. I watched her with a kind of awe. This moment meant something, although I didn't know what.

'Just relax, make yourself at home,' I said. My voice sounded far too loud. I was practically shouting. 'So, would you like a drink?' My voice was still wrong.

'Yeah, that'd be nice. What have you got?' Sophie half-looked up at me.

'Well, I always keep a bottle of wine in my room,' I lied. 'So there should be one here, somewhere.' I pretended to root about in my wardrobe. But I knew exactly

85

where the wine was. I'd only bought it from Sainsbury's two hours ago. 'Yeah, here we go.' I produced the bottle and two wine glasses. 'Medium dry all right?'

'Yes, whatever.'

I opened the wine with something of a flourish. Then I poured out two glasses. I took a sip, then another. 'It doesn't taste right,' I said. 'It's too warm for a start, isn't it?'

'No, mine's . . .' began Sophie.

But I was already tearing downstairs for some ice.

'There we go,' I said, plopping some ice into her glass. I gulped my wine down without even tasting it. Then I paced around my room, trying to find some things I thought might entertain her.

I showed her my skiing goggles, even though I've never gone skiing in my life. Dementedly, I searched around for other things that would let her see what a wild and wacky and deeply fascinating guy I was.

Finally I pulled out my toy sword and shield. At once, Sophie grabbed the shield. 'I like this,' she said.

'Now come on, Sophie, you don't hold it out like that,' I said. 'You've got to hold it much closer to yourself . . . yeah, that's it. Now you're invincible.'

Sophie grinned at me. 'That's good to know . . . I can just see you playing with all this.'

'Can you?' I felt both pleased and embarrassed. 'Yeah,

when I was younger I was a real stuntboy. If you're lucky I might show you my knight's helmet later.'

'You know how to tempt a girl, don't you?' said Sophie with a saucy smile. We were both starting to relax properly now.

Next we went through my CD collection. At first I just showed her the good stuff. But then I dug out some really dodgy tapes that I'd bought when I was about four days old. She and I were both sitting cross-legged on the floor, laughing at my appalling taste when my mum called up, 'How are you getting on with the play, Ben?'

I grinned at Sophie. We hadn't even looked at the play yet. 'It's going really well,' I called. 'Sophie's got loads of ideas.' She giggled at that.

'Well, we're going to bed soon,' said Mum. 'Goodnight, Sophie. Goodnight, Ben.' I winced. Subtlety was not my mum's strong point.

'Should I go?' asked Sophie.

'No, no, stay. Stay all night – stay all year, if you like.' But then it hit me, she was only fifteen. It was as if I couldn't hold that fact in my head. Even when I'd glimpsed her around school, in that vomit-yellow school uniform, she still seemed as if she was wearing a disguise, pretending to be a fifth year.

'Your parents won't mind, will they?' I asked.

Sophie shrugged her shoulders. There was an edge to

her voice now. 'They don't like me being out late, but they won't say anything, especially after . . .' She raised her now unbandaged wrists almost proudly. Then she smiled confidingly. 'They're afraid to do anything to upset me now. Nick might try and stir things up, though.'

'You and your brother . . .' I hesitated.

'Yes.' She smiled but more to herself than me.

'You and he don't get on, do you?'

'We do and we don't,' said Sophie. 'When it's just him and me we get on fine. He can be really nice . . . and quite protective of me in a funny way. But as soon as we're with other people he's totally different. It's like we're in a competition.' She gave a short laugh. 'He says I take all his glory, whatever that means.'

'He told me you went out with one of his mates,' I said.

'I can't believe he told you that,' Sophie looked thrown for a moment, 'but then he made such a big deal about it at the time.' She shook her head in amazement. 'I went out with him once, that's all. We went to the cinema. I didn't even like him, really. I think I was just flattered because, well, I'm not exactly skinny now but when I was younger I was really fat.'

'All girls think they're really fat,' I said, dismissively.

'But I really was,' said Sophie. 'I mean, at school every

year we used to get weighed and all our weights were put on a chart. And I knew I'd be the heaviest. So I always had to be sick or do something to get sent home, because I couldn't bear to see my name up there. But everyone knew. Anyway, these other girls would come up to me: "You're fatter than me." ' She smiled. 'That day felt like a year and I'd be sweating so much . . . I must have lost a stone just sweating about it.'

'It was probably only puppy fat. I hate skinny girls, anyhow,' I said. Then I added, 'I was a real geek when I was younger.'

She grinned cheekily. 'Haven't changed much, then.'

I got up. 'You want to see how much I've changed, this photo of me carries a government health warning.' I rooted around in one of my drawers. 'Have to keep the picture hidden away,' I said. 'Here, look at this and weep.'

Sophie took the photo. 'Your clothes . . . they're a bit high fashion, aren't they?' She started to laugh.

'What are you saying about my let's-hang-out-in-McDonald's clothes?'

'No, I like them, honestly.' We were both laughing now.

Then she said suddenly, 'Can I ask you something?'

'Sure.'

'Have you got any candles?'

'I'm not certain. Why?'

'No, it's just I like candles. They create a good atmosphere . . .'

I was on my feet right away. 'I'll get some,' I said. And I rooted some out from downstairs, ignoring my mum's curious looks as I did so.

Sophie watched me appreciatively. 'I don't know why I love candles,' she said, 'but they always make me feel warm and cosy and safe . . . and intimate.'

'Every time you're round here I shall have candles waiting for you.'

Later we sat together on the carpet, peering at my script. Her legs were pressing tightly against mine. I'd gaze at those soft lips and deep green eyes. Then I'd get a whiff of her perfume. And I knew that even when I was ninety-four and shrivelling away like an old prune, one sniff of that perfume would set my heart racing. I might die as a result of so much excitement. But what the hell, I'd die in the throes of ecstasy!

At first I couldn't really concentrate on what she was saying but then she said, 'I've thought of a title for the play. You'll probably hate it: *The Dreams Are Calling*.'

I started writing it down, my mind still far away. Then I looked at it. 'It's a brilliant title.'

'Really?' She sounded pleased.

'What made you think of it?'

'I don't know. I just thought of the old man watching the girl he loved exactly as she was, all those years ago . . . that would kill me.'

'In the end, it kills him,' I said.

'Yeah, but the dream takes pity on him – and lets him go back.'

'I think you understand the play better than me.'

'I do like it,' she said. 'Especially your ending, it's so moving.'

'Well, in a way, you're in it,' I said, very softly.

'Am I – you mean, the girl being called Sophie and all that?'

'Not just that,' I murmured.

'Well, that's a real compliment,' she whispered. Then she leant across, took the remains of the ice cube out of her glass and started sucking it. Normally if a girl did that, I'd think I was going out with a nine-year-old. But when Sophie did it, it just added to her charm, somehow. 'Of course,' she said, 'Sophie in the play has got blonde hair.'

I shrugged my shoulders. 'That's nothing.'

'No,' Sophie agreed. 'Anyway, I'm really proud of you. This play is going to be wonderful.'

'If you're there, it will be,' I said.

She looked puzzled. 'Me, why?'

'Because you named it, you understand. Really the

play should have your name on it, too.' Underneath my name I wrote, 'With special thanks to Sophie Doyle.'

'No, don't,' she said. 'I'm just happy to have helped.'

'Too late, it's done.' Then, still staring down at the script, I murmured, 'I want your name beside mine . . . and I want you there with me next week. I need you there, please.'

'Do you really?' Her voice fell away for a moment. 'All right, Ben, I'll be there.'

Later I walked her home. And outside her house I said, 'Ring me then.'

And she said, 'When?' Just one word. But I loved the way she said it, as if she wanted to see me again as soon as possible.

Unfortunately, I blew it, by replying, 'Whenever.' And all the way home I worried that I'd sounded too flippant. Why hadn't I said, 'Very soon.'

I wanted to ring up and say it to her right then at two o'clock in the morning. Instead, I went back upstairs to my bedroom. Sometimes, I quite like reclaiming my room after my friends have left. But tonight was different. I sat down on my bed. The candle was still flickering away. And her perfume . . . I'm sure I could still smell it. I could hear her voice, too, saying, 'I'm really proud of you. This play is going to be wonderful.' And there she was sitting so close to me on the carpet . . . My empty room was no longer empty.

She was everywhere.

The following day Sophie rang me and arranged to go to the sixth-form drama meeting with me. As soon as we walked into the hall there were definite murmurings. What could a fifth-year be doing at a sixth-form club? People can be so pathetic sometimes. That's why, when Ernie asked me to introduce the play, I spent all the time talking about Sophie and her contribution. 'Without her help and inspiration,' I said, 'there probably wouldn't be a play. I wanted you all to know that.'

I looked across at Sophie. She was sitting with her arms wrapped around herself. But I knew she was pleased I'd said that.

The play itself was a big success. Everyone seemed amazed I'd written it. 'It's not at all the sort of play I'd imagine you'd write,' said Vanessa, which just showed how little she really knew me.

Ernie had a few suggestions for improvement – mainly cuts; it was four minutes too long. But he also said the play had 'great potential' and he would definitely enter it for the competition.

It was then I had a brilliant idea. I was amazed I hadn't thought of it before.

4 . . . Sophie's Big Chance

I'd planned to tell Sophie my great idea the following evening. She'd never been up to the top of Windmill Hill at night before and it seemed the ideal setting. But instead, I got sidetracked by a bombshell from my parents: my dad said to me, 'We've got some surprising news for you . . . your mum's pregnant.'

It had been bad enough last time when Glen was born: all the mess and upheaval and that horrible baby smell which just took over the house. Not to mention the way I kept getting lumbered with all those extra jobs ('No, don't worry, Ben will do that.').

But now they were far too old to be having babies. Mum was forty, Dad forty-one. It was my turn next. I felt as if they were taking something away from me: babies belonged to the young. Then I started wondering what would happen to my room. The baby was due at the end of August and there were only three bedrooms, so I supposed my going to university in September was very handy for them. When I returned at Christmas I was sure I'd find my room taken over.

My mum and dad seemed on a real high about the whole thing. And when Glen was told 'there was a baby growing inside Mummy's tummy', he went over and kissed Mum's tummy and said, 'Hello, baby.' Everyone was happy about it except me. So I bottled up all my negative reactions until I saw Sophie. Sitting beside her at the top of Windmill Hill I poured out my true feelings. It was a relief just to say it all. She didn't interrupt me once, just listened really intently. Finally, I said, 'Thanks for letting me go on like this. It must be very boring for you.'

'No, not at all,' she said. 'I'm glad you told me, especially as ... well, you've got this very polished surface, and you don't like anyone to see behind that surface. You don't really trust many people, do you?'

I was startled. 'No, I suppose I don't.'

'I know I don't,' said Sophie, with surprising force.

'Do you trust anyone?' I asked.

She hesitated.

'Do you trust me?' I persisted.

'Yes, I do,' she said quietly.

'Ah, you're only saying that,' I said, mock-seriously. 'You won't let me see behind *your* polished surface, will you?'

She picked up my light tone. 'Oh, I might.' Then she added, 'Ask me something. Anything.'

'What, now?'

'Yes, go on.'

Of course my mind went totally blank. 'All right, when did you first fancy me? No, don't answer that,' I added quickly, 'that was just a joke. OK, in your bedroom there's only one photograph: a really old one, of this woman smiling. Is that your nan? There, that's an amazing question, isn't it?'

'Mind-blowing. And actually, it isn't my nan.'

'The mystery deepens.'

'No, she's . . .' And for just a second Sophie hesitated. 'I suppose you could say I adopted her.'

I looked at her questioningly. 'I'm intrigued now.'

'Well, what happened was: where we lived before there was an old people's home very near and this friend of mine and her mum used to visit regularly, and one day I went too. We were supposed to read aloud to the old ladies so I went over to one in the corner and as soon as I started reading she closed her eyes. I was about to get up when she suddenly opened her eyes and asked me where

I'd got my jacket from as it was very nice. Then we got talking. And although she was tiny and very frail she had smiling eyes and was really interested in what I was doing. Nora . . . that was her name. And I went back to see her quite a lot.

'I remember once going to visit her on a bank holiday and I thought the place would be packed with family visiting. And do you know, there wasn't one visitor there. Not one. Just the old ladies imprisoned in their chairs as usual, and all this emptiness around them . . . I thought that was terrible.' She stared ahead of her, as if lost in thought for a moment. 'She gave me that picture when I told her I was leaving, insisted I took it. I often think about her.' She turned towards me. 'OK, your turn, tell me about the old people in your life.'

I considered this. 'I did like my grandad especially as he lived by the sea. He died when I was about ten. But I can remember him quite clearly: especially at night walking along the seafront when he used to tell me stories about these sea creatures that were brought in by the tide, yet they were so magical they never left any trace in the sand . . .'

I stopped. The moon was shining behind the clouds. And its light caught the top of Sophie's hair, making it glow softly. I leant forward and kissed her on the cheek. I moved my lips nearer to hers. That was quite a bashful kiss. Then I kissed her on the lips again. I opened my mouth a little, she opened hers and the kiss just surged on and on, until I felt her shiver. 'Are you cold?' I asked.

'No, not really.'

I put my arm around her and I felt her body pressing against mine. 'Sophie,' I whispered.

'What?'

I wasn't sure. I just knew I wanted to say something astounding to her. In the end, I whispered, 'You're the best.'

'So are you,' she whispered.

And that was when I told her my great idea.

They were casting for my play next week and I wasn't too excited about the thought of all those weeks of rehearsals, without Sophie. I needed her there beside me. At first I had wondered about making her some kind of consultant. But then came the brain-wave: Sophie could be 'Sophie Stevens'. It wasn't a very big part and Ernie had decided that both the girl's scenes could be recorded on video so it wouldn't matter that Sophie was inexperienced. I would help coach her and I was a pretty dead cert to play the old man. So the last scene would feature Sophie and me, the other side of the screen in black and white, disappearing into our happy ending. Sophie had to be in that scene. Anyone else was unthinkable.

So I told her, 'We're discussing casting our play

tomorrow and I'm going to propose you should be in it.'

She sat up shocked. 'Me, why?'

'Because you'd be terrible. What do you mean, why?'

'But I'm not even a sixth-former.'

'That doesn't matter. What matters is, you're the best person to play Sophie.'

'I've never acted in my life,' she gasped.

'So much the better,' I said.

'No, I don't think so. I get nervous.'

'All your scenes would be recorded.'

'Would they?' There was a pause. 'But I don't know if I'll be any good.'

'You will. Trust me. I know talent . . . I'll help you . . . Come on.'

'I don't know.'

'Look, all you've got to do is audition. If you're really terrible you won't get the part, that's all. But I know you'll be brilliant. You understand this girl. You helped with some of the dialogue.'

'Did I?' She sounded dazed. 'I wondered how much I really helped you.'

'Don't be silly, I couldn't have written this play without you, and if you're not in it, well, it won't be any good.'

'All right,' she said, finally. 'I'll audition. Just don't be too disappointed if I'm rubbish.'

*

Next day the drama group sat round in a circle, while Ernie read out the nominations. Three boys (the only other boys in the group) were auditioning for Alex but my name was the only one down for the old man.

'The part is yours, Ben,' said Ernie.

I think the group felt as I'd written the play I deserved the part I wanted.

There were six nominations for Katie – including Vanessa – and five for Sophie Stevens, ending with Sophie's. At once there was an eruption from Andrea Carter. I should have expected that. She was a strange girl: always storming off in a huff about nothing. 'Who put a fifth-year's name down for one of our parts?' she demanded.

'I did,' I said, quietly.

'Why?' she demanded.

'Why not? I thought drama was supposed to open us up to other people. All I'm asking is that Sophie be given a chance.'

'Maybe we should vote on it,' said Ernie.

'That's fair,' said Andrea.

Yes, it was very fair. And I'm a keen believer in democracy but I also knew I'd definitely lose so I said, 'No, I'm not voting on it. This is my play and if Sophie is not allowed to audition, then I'll take my play away.'

There was a stunned silence. I was pretty stunned

myself but I'd been pushed into taking such an extreme position.

'You can't do that,' said Andrea.

'Yes I can,' I said. And then in an effort to justify myself, I added, 'What you're forgetting is, if it weren't for Sophie there wouldn't be any play.'

'But she's not a sixth-former,' cried Andrea.

'So what. You're all so ageist.' I darted a glance at Ernie, knowing this was the kind of language that hooked him. He liked to think he was so 'right on'. 'The sixth-form drama group is not some élite clique, it's . . . a state of mind.'

Andrea just glared at me. 'So, because it's your play we've all got to bow down and do whatever you say.' Then she turned away from me, and said in the loudest whisper possible, 'Well, we all know about the director's couch, don't we.'

That was stingingly nasty. No wonder it made my eyes smart. I hate people making cracks about me, even people I don't respect like Andrea Carter. And this time it involved Sophie too. That was unforgivable. I haven't hated anyone for years as I hated Andrea Carter then but I didn't respond. I just put my face into neutral.

'I don't think that was a very helpful comment,' said Ernie.

Vanessa added quietly, 'As Sophie had such a hand in the play, I think she should be given a chance to audition.' I gave her a grateful glance.

'Might I make a proposal to be debated?' said Ernie. 'We recognise Sophie's help with the play by letting her audition, but in addition to the read-through, we add an improvisation section.'

'I think that's a good idea,' said Laura, one of the leaders of the group. And suddenly there were smiles all around. I knew what they were thinking: they did improvisations every week, so they had a big advantage over Sophie. But we'd show them. A little bit of coaching from me and Sophie would leave all these behind at the starting post, because she had natural talent.

'But it's still not fair,' wailed Andrea, 'because he's picking the actors.' She pointed at me.

'We're both picking the actors,' said Ernie, with surprising force. 'It will be a joint decision.'

That calmed things down a bit. Although there was still indignant whispering – especially from Andrea's corner. But I'd won that round: Sophie would go to the audition. Part of me was applauding wildly. The other part felt vulnerable, exposed, alone. When the group first read my play I was practically a hero. Now you couldn't give my shares away; I was a pathetic egomaniac, who was foolishly trying to put his little girlfriend into a sixth-form play. My ears would be burning tonight and for many nights to come. Still, it didn't seem too high a price to pay. Not when you considered the catastrophic alternative.

Afterwards, Vanessa came over. I thanked her for her support. 'I didn't think I had a friend in the world out there,' I said.

'Aaah, poor Ben,' said Vanessa softly and she gave me a little hug.

'What they didn't see is I wanted Sophie in the play because she'd be good. That's all.'

'Mmm,' said Vanessa, rather absently. She gave me a strange smile. 'Still, if someone had fought for me the way you fought for Sophie, I'd be so happy . . . I do like your play, and I think I understand Katie. I'll have to give you my theories about her sometime. No, I think it's a very good play and I'd like to be in it, but that's not a hint.' She laughed.

'No, of course not.' I laughed too.

'But really, I need something like this play. I mean, I'm hardly talking to my stepdad, and Nick – well, I love him to bits but he's everywhere. And sometimes I can't breathe . . . I think he misses seeing you. He doesn't say anything but I think he does.'

I smiled embarrassedly then said, 'Don't tell Sophie about all the fuss today, will you?'

'Of course I won't,' Vanessa replied. 'But she may find out. You know what this school's like for gossip.'

And somehow, Sophie did find out.

We were in my bedroom, by candlelight, when she said, 'Your drama group don't want me in this play, do they?'

'What makes you say that?'

'Come on, Ben, they don't.'

'All right, there's a couple . . .'

'Like the whole group.'

'No, not at all. Vanessa supports you.' I hesitated.

'One person.' She laughed. 'I mean, wow.' Then she added, 'You can't blame them. I mean, I'm not even in the group.'

'You helped with the play.'

'Not really.' She looked away. 'All I did was read it and make a few poxy suggestions . . . I didn't do anything. Yet everyone in my form keeps coming up to me: "Is it true you inspired a play and you're going to be in it?" All this fuss is making me feel paranoid.'

'About what?'

'I don't know. They're all expecting . . . . I'm not that good. Really, I'm not.'

'So you're going to throw it all away because of a few jealous people.' My head was throbbing furiously. 'But that's OK, let Andrea take your part and totally sabotage

104

the play . . . I don't expect I'll even bother to go and see it.' I stood up, angrily. 'You're really annoying me tonight.'

She stared at me. 'Why?'

'Because you've got so much talent and yet you won't do anything, because you're afraid of what people might say.'

'No, I'm not,' she said, with sudden force. 'I do what I want to do. And no one can stop me. No one.' Then she looked up at me without saying anything. I held the gaze. It just went on and on, until finally, she said, softly, 'All right.'

'You don't have to.'

'I know. I want to.'

'And if jealous people say any more things . . . and they will . . .'

She shrugged her shoulders. 'I don't care. The only person I listen to is you, anyway.'

It was then I had such a rush of feeling for Sophie, it left me breathless. In a way it was scary. For the first time in my life I was putting someone ahead of me. Before Sophie, I was a pretty selfish person. I can remember going down the town to buy my mum a birthday present and then spending all my money on me. But in the days leading up to the audition I put everything else on hold. And each night I went through Sophie's scenes with her. She learnt the lines quickly and her voice was good. The only thing that worried me was her walk. In truth, it was the only unattractive thing about her. It was a rather dumpy, awkward walk. I tried subtly to encourage Sophie to move more slowly, more elegantly. We also practised some improvisation pieces. Sometimes Sophie would say something and it sounded so funny we'd both have a pain from laughing so much.

Then it was the day of the auditions, on St Valentine's Day. I went into the hall. They were all there, waiting – all except Sophie. I'd been looking for her all day. Normally, Sophie and I made a point of not speaking at school. But today I wanted to wish her luck. Maybe she'd lost her nerve. Was this all too much for her? But then the door opened and there she was and as she walked over to me I stuttered, 'Your hair.'

'Yeah, I know.' She laughed faintly. 'I just felt like a change and I thought, why not. What do . . .'

'You look wonderful,' I interrupted. And that was an understatement. Often when girls dye their hair blonde, it looks cheap and fake. With Sophie, it highlighted her beauty and made her look more mysterious and older. She could easily pass for twenty now.

I smiled. 'Now you are Sophie. I mean Sophie in the play.'

'My mum thought I was mad,' she said. 'But I wanted to.'

I put out my hand. 'You're the best,' I whispered.

'So are you,' she whispered back.

Then Ernie arrived and announced there would be group improvisations, followed by individual auditions. Last night, when I'd asked Sophie if she was nervous she'd just laughed. But now she was frowning with concentration, biting the side of her lip. She looked like a little child waiting to go into the dentist's surgery. I wanted to put my arm around her. I so wanted to tell her she had the part.

The improvisation group had to pretend they were on a train and take on different characters. Sophie played a rather stern woman who complained that someone was smoking in a non-smoking compartment. At first she was too quiet and still moved a little awkwardly but, as she gained confidence, she improved and even got a few laughs at the end. I thought she did really well.

Then the audition followed. Andrea was appalling. She shouted her lines, which was totally wrong. If she played 'Sophie' she'd wreck the whole thing. Sophie was the last person to audition. She came forward biting her thumb. I tried to signal to her not to do that as Ernie noticed those things. Then came her scene: her lover is dead and her family have told her to forget him. 'They told me to forget him,' began Sophie, with that tremor in her voice. She became contemptuous. 'They understand so little . . .' Her voice rose, just as I'd coached her and then she brought something to those words I'd never heard before: a terrible sad desperation. 'Forgetting him, would be like forgetting myself.' You had to lean forward to hear her last words: 'I'll be waiting . . . I'll wait for ever for you.'

I stared at her and thought, soon, she'll be saying those words on video and I'll be there with her. At the end of the play we'll leave together. And one day we'll be showing that video to our grandchildren. I knew I was getting carried away. But what the hell, she'd been wonderful up there: blindingly, blazingly, wonderful.

Ernie and I went off to confer in his office, more like a cupboard actually, where theatre posters dangled precariously on the walls, as if uncertain whether to make that dizzying jump on to the carpet or not. There was a funny smell too; an unedifying cocktail of sweat and tobacco. But it wasn't the smell which made me feel sick, it was nerves, and shame. This was my play. MY PLAY. And yet, I really didn't care who played Alex or Katie. All I could think about was . . .

'And now "Sophie",' said Ernie. I snapped back to life. 'There were two auditions which stood out for me,' he went on. 'Sophie and Emma.'

EMMA. To be honest, I'd forgotten she'd even

existed. 'Emma was all right,' I said, slowly, 'but I didn't think she was especially memorable.'

'Mmmm,' mused Ernie. 'I thought Emma moved very well, very graceful. Sophie was rather clumsy, especially in the improvisation section and her voice needs training. Still . . .' He paused, 'I did think Sophie was remarkable.'

I looked across at him and felt that flash of comrade-ship I normally only feel when I meet a fellow Spurs' supporter. He saw what I saw. I blurted out, 'I thought she was totally brilliant. She was "Sophie".' Immediately I wished I hadn't said that.

Ernie gave me a look, kindly but rather sad as he said carefully, 'So you'd be happy with Sophie in that role?'

After Ernie announced the results Sophie rushed over to me. 'I was so nervous. I didn't want to let you down.'

'You certainly haven't done that,' I said.

We smiled at each other. 'Without you,' said Sophie, 'and all those long nights of coaching in your bedroom . . .' She grinned cheekily, then added softly, 'I owe it all to you.'

'Stick with me,' I said, 'and I'll show you all the heights. One day the whole world will be asking for your autograph.'

There was no time to say anything else, as *some* (note

my emphasis here) of the drama group were congratulating Sophie. Vanessa gave Sophie a hug. Then she gave me a rather weary smile. I knew she was disappointed she hadn't been picked to play Katie.

'It was a close thing,' I said. And actually, Vanessa had been quite good. But Ernie thought Laura had a stronger stage presence, so we picked her instead.

'I could have done with some of your extra coaching,' said Vanessa. She said this as a kind of joke, but neither of us was laughing. She thought I'd let her down. But I couldn't have given her the part just because she was a friend. That wouldn't be fair. Sophie had gained the part because she was so good. It was nothing to do with me pulling strings. Surely Vanessa could see that. Vanessa sighed. 'Actually, I don't think I could have taken on the role anyway. I'm just so busy these days.' And that night Vanessa left the drama group. So did two other girls.

There was no time to say any more to Sophie as she went off with Vanessa shortly afterwards: chauffeur Nick was waiting faithfully outside. But I declined the offer of a lift and told Sophie I'd ring her later. I had something important to do.

3 . . . Let Me Be Free of Her

There were two other guys in the flower shop. We gave each other furtive smiles. We were on alien territory. Only a special emergency, like Valentine's Day, could bring us in here.

I remembered the wild excitement that had arisen when Ryan gave Sophie those roses. At first I was going to give her twelve red roses to prove how deeply committed I was. But then I decided to make it eleven red roses and one white rose; that still showed how much stronger my love was than Ryan's, yet, it also gave her something to work for, a little challenge.

I walked quickly home, praying no one would see me, as I felt a bit of a prat carrying those roses. I decided I'd deposit them on my bed and just write on the card:

'Congratulations on being "Sophie". Much love, Ben.'
She alone would know the double meaning.

Just as I was walking up my drive, Dad drove in. He got out of the car and grinned at me. 'Are these for me, Ben? You shouldn't.'

I cringed embarrassedly. 'I got these for Sophie. She's just won a part in my play,' I said, to the pavement.

'Excellent, excellent,' said Dad. Then he gave a sly, confiding smile. 'But weren't you the judge?'

'One of the judges,' I snapped.

'Oh, yes. Ah, right,' he said.

Then Mum was in the doorway. 'You're home early.'

'It was such a nice evening, I just walked out of the office.' He looked around for Glen, who, normally, would be running around him, clapping his hands, yelling, 'My daddy's home! My daddy's home!'

As if reading his thoughts, Mum said, 'Glen is at his friend Josh's party. I told you this morning.'

'Of course you did.' He produced a small bunch of red roses. 'These are for you.'

'And I thought you'd forgotten.' Mum looked genuinely pleased. She kissed Dad on the cheek.

'Not that I don't feel totally outclassed by my son here.'

Mum smiled faintly at me. 'I suppose those are for Sophie.'

'She's won a part in my play. These are to congratulate her,' I mumbled, before exiting upstairs.

In the past, whenever I'd gone out with a girl, I'd always played it to my family as just a friendship. And once at my house, when a girl finished with me after she'd forgiven her ex-boyfriend, she left so suddenly my parents knew something was wrong. But when I went into the kitchen I had a real don't-ask-me-about-it look on my face, as they were the last people I wanted to talk about this with. And that was nothing against my parents. Not at all. It was just – well, when you get to be twelve or thirteen you don't let your parents see you in the nude any more. And it's exactly the same with girls: that part of your life has to be secret from them. That's why I hated my mum and dad catching me with those flowers. I only hoped they'd have the good sense to forget the whole thing. But a few minutes later Dad called upstairs, 'Ben, have you got a minute?'

'I've just made some tea,' said Mum. She and Dad were sitting on the couch together. Since the news about the baby they'd been very 'lovey' with each other.

'No tea for me, thanks,' I said. I sat down on the chair opposite them. I felt awkward, maybe because they looked like an interview panel. So what was I to be interviewed about?

Dad smiled at me. 'It's good news about Sophie being in your play, isn't it?'

Mum nodded and smiled too. There was something forced about this. It felt like an overture to something much more ominous.

'You've been seeing quite a lot of Sophie lately, haven't you?' said Mum. Immediately I felt a wave of anger: I really didn't want to talk about Sophie with them. Not like this, anyhow.

'And that's great,' Mum went on. 'She's a nice girl and we're happy for you and . . . I know bedrooms have changed since my day. My bedroom was just somewhere I slept, but now it's your own special place where you take your friends and that's fine.' She hesitated. 'But I have to say, we don't like you wandering around at one in the morning.'

'I don't wander around,' I said. 'I see Sophie home and she lives about five minutes away.'

'You're gone more than five minutes,' said Mum. 'I know, because I lie awake counting all the cracks on the wallpaper. I can't sleep until I hear you get in.'

'And your mum needs her sleep, especially now,' said Dad.

'OK, I'll come in more quietly,' I said.

'But I also see the lights go on.'

'How can you, when you're upstairs,' I said. 'But that's

OK, don't worry, I won't put any lights on when I come in, either.'

'Don't be silly.' Mum smiled. 'It's all right for your dad, he sleeps through anything. But I . . . I worry about you being set upon in the streets.'

I softened at this and said, quite gently, 'Mum, there's no one about at that time. It's probably safer than in the day.'

'And what do Sophie's parents think about her coming in late every night?' went on Mum.

'They don't mind at all,' I said. Actually, Sophie had told me her parents had started making comments about her late nights. But I wasn't going to admit that here.

Then it was Dad's turn again. 'The thing is, Ben, we all have to get up for work, so we think it's fair to set some restrictions. From now on we'd like you to be in by half-past eleven.'

'Half-past eleven,' I echoed, disbelievingly.

'That seems a reasonable deadline for workdays. Weekends are negotiable.'

I stared at him, stunned. So now when I was out with Sophie I'd have to be looking at my watch all the time. Got to be home by half-past eleven, Sophie, or Mummy and Daddy will be cross with me. I was eighteen, for goodness sake.

'Don't forget, you've got a very busy time ahead of

you,' declared Mum. 'What with your exams and . . . and that's why we want you to enjoy yourself, but keep your options open, too.'

I stared at her suspiciously. Now what was she trying to say?

'What do you mean, keep my options open?' I asked.

Mum and Dad looked at each other: a real shall-we-give-it-to-him look. I hate it when people do that; it's guaranteed to make you feel excluded.

'We're just thinking about you,' said Mum, slowly, 'and we don't want you to take on more than you can handle.'

I shrugged my shoulders. 'I haven't a clue what you're talking about.' But I could make a pretty good guess.

Mum went on, 'All we're saying is, you're going to be very busy and will need your wits about you . . . so you don't want any distractions.'

'Distractions.' I pounced on the word.

'What we mean, is,' said Mum, slowly, 'we know you're seeing a lot of Sophie these days and that's fine. She's a very nice girl, and we both like her. But . . .' That 'but' hung about ominously. 'But we're concerned that you and she are going to get bogged down into something you hadn't bargained for.'

I glared at Mum. Don't poison this, I thought. Don't twist Sophie and me into some big problem. PLEASE.

'You and she seem to have become very serious so quickly,' said Mum. 'I mean, that's just my impression, how it appears.' She gave an apology of a laugh. 'Obviously, I'm not upstairs with you.'

'Oh, well, we'll put a seat in for you, if you like,' I said.

'There's no need for that tone,' snapped Dad. But they were interfering in things they didn't understand and weren't anything to do with them. 'We're only trying to help you,' said Dad. 'And we can see danger.'

'Danger,' I murmured scornfully. I was seeing a girl not joining the Mafia.

'We just don't want to see you throw away everything you've worked for,' said Dad. 'And it can happen. It does happen. There's this chap at work, his son James is a year older than you. Maybe you've heard me mention him.' I shrugged my shoulders. I didn't know or care if I'd heard James's name or not. 'Well, this time last year, James was doing his A levels and he was all set for success, then he met this girl: let her take up all his time, got rotten grades, missed his university place and then broke up with the girl, anyway.' Dad paused significantly.

'Wow, what an amazing story,' I said.

'All right,' began Dad.

'No, really, thank you for sharing that with me. I'll probably think about that story for the rest of my life.' If there was one thing Dad didn't appreciate from me, it was sarcasm. It always touched a nerve and that was exactly what I wanted to do. I felt humiliated.

For a moment Dad sat there clenching his teeth, as if desperately reining in his anger and then he said, with heavy-handed reasonableness, 'We don't want to cramp your style in any way and we recognise you're eighteen. All we're asking is that you show a little more consideration at night and – we're suggesting, at this busy time of your life, you cool it a little with Sophie.'

I was clenching my teeth now. 'Thanks for your very helpful advice. All right if I ring Sophie now?'

Mum started gathering up the teacups. 'You're not working as hard as you used to, I know that. You'll be lucky even to pass your A levels the way you're going on, let alone get the grades you want.' She sighed and turned to Dad. 'Still, sometimes you have to let people get on with it and learn by their own mistakes.'

I didn't trust myself to reply to that. Instead, I stalked off to the hallway. I stood in front of the phone, angered and bewildered by my parents' attitude. I had always got on well with them even three or four years ago, when everyone else was having hassle with their parents.

But tonight, they'd let me down. They'd blundered past my 'keep out' signs and driven a wedge between me and them.

I started dialling Sophie's number.

'Hello.' I never needed to say who I was now.

'Ben . . . hi . . . hi.' I'd expected her to be elated after her triumph at the drama club. Instead, her voice sounded oddly muffled.

'Are you OK?'

'Yeah, oh yeah, I'm fine.' But she still sounded strange.

'Can you talk?' I asked. For if Nick or her parents were near she'd just clam up.

'No, it's just . . . I've got a guest here at the moment.'

A guest. What an oddly formal way of putting it.

'So, who's your guest?' I asked, slightly amused.

'Actually, it's Ryan.'

At once, my heart started pounding. 'How long's he been there?'

'When I got back he was waiting for me in his car. I wasn't expecting him at all. He was just there. It was weird.' She sounded disorientated.

I was finding it hard to control my voice now. 'So how much longer is he staying there, the rest of the night or . . .?'

'No, no. Look, Ben, I'll be round when I can . . . soon. I'll see you then, OK?'

Before I could reply she'd gone. Not that she'd ever really been with me during that conversation. One visit from Ryan and I was forgotten. All my time with Sophie was just wiped out. He had immaculate timing. No doubt he'd come round with a suitably wonderful Valentine's Day present: some new gimmick. And she'd been as charmed as she had been by his roses.

What was he doing round there? Whatever it was, he couldn't be trusted. I wanted to ring her back and tell her that. But I decided it would sound better coming from someone else. I rang Jenny.

She answered the phone, sounding hoarse and breathless, as usual. 'Hello.'

'Hi, Jenny, how are you?'

Her voice became plaintive. 'I haven't been very well.'

'Oh, yeah. Simon said you'd had a bad cold.'

'You didn't ring up to see how I was though, did you – you big poo.'

I immediately felt guilty. 'I meant to. Sorry.'

'So you should be. And I didn't have a cold, I had acute inflammation of the lungs.'

'Oh, you would, wouldn't you? You couldn't have something normal, like a cold.'

She started to laugh. 'Don't take the mickey. I've had to have antibiotics and everything. Anyway, what do you want?'

'To tell you some good news and some bad news. The good news is, that Sophie's got a part in my play.'

'Oh, that's nice. Don't forget to get us tickets, will you?'

'I won't. The competitions's the end of May.'

'Whenever, wherever, we'll be there. It's exciting. And, I suppose the bad news is, you're acting in the play, too.'

'No . . .' I hesitated.

'It's nothing really awful, is it?' asked Jenny.

'I'll tell you what it is.' My voice was starting to rise. 'Ryan's just turned up round Sophie's house.'

'Who's Ryan?'

'Her ex-boyfriend, the one who dumped her,' I said, impatiently.

'Oh yes. I'd just forgotten for a minute. So what's he doing round there? I thought he was seeing someone else, his boss, wasn't it?'

'That's right. Sophie really doesn't need this at the moment, just when she's sorting her life out and starting to get somewhere. I mean, this part in the play is a major break for her. She was just brilliant at the audition.'

'Mmm,' said Jenny.

'And now this Ryan is just going to cause Sophie more grief.' Suddenly, I was aware that I was shouting. I tried to lower my voice. 'Look, will you speak to her, Jen, warn her?' There was a definite pause on the other end of the line. 'Jen, are you still there?'

'Yes, I'm thinking.' Her voice softened. 'I don't think I can do that.'

'Why not?' I was rudely indignant.

'Well, I hardly know her, really. I can't just ring her up and start giving her advice. I know everyone thinks I'm mighty-mouth, and I'm always saying things I shouldn't. If she rang me, that would be different, but . . . no.'

'That's all right then. Don't worry,' I snapped.

'Don't get huffy with me, Ben, I want to help.'

'It sounds like it.'

'Now, that's out of order, that's unfair.'

'I know,' I said quietly.

'Ben, I hope you don't mind me asking, but what are you and Sophie? Are you just good friends, or are you actually going out together, or what?'

'Well, at first I was helping Sophie and since then we've just got closer.' I stopped. I'd just pictured us becoming closer until finally we'd be so entwined that nothing could tear us apart. That was my dream. The reality was very different: Sophie getting back together with Ryan and me standing on the sidelines as Sophie's loyal friend, Mr Nice Guy, smiling generously while Sophie and Ryan disappeared into the sunset. My insides twisted with anger.

Jenny said, 'I do know Sophie likes you very much.'

'Oh yeah, she likes me all right, but only as a friend. It's Ryan who she wants . . .'

'No, come on, Ben, you don't know that. She hasn't told you that.'

'She didn't need to. It was there in her voice. She couldn't wait for me to get off the phone.'

'It takes time to get over people.'

'Oh yeah, sure. I'll tell you what it is, shall I? All girls go for guys like Ron the roofer who mess them around. That's what you love.'

'No, we don't. No way.'

'Yes, you do. It gives you a fake feeling of danger or something. While, if guys are nice, then it's like they've got a disease. Avoid them at all costs.'

'Ben, don't talk like that. All my girl friends think you're really nice-looking, and they . . .'

'But I've spent all this time on her and all for what?' I was practically crying on the phone and a part of me was watching myself in horror.

'Ben, listen to me. Look, you have helped Sophie a lot, but sometimes you can try too hard.'

'None of you are worth it. None of you.'

'If I were round your house, I'd hit you for saying that.'

'I'm sorry,' I said.

'Oh, shut up,' said Jenny cheerfully.

That made me laugh, relaxed us both. Then Jenny said, 'Simon was saying to me, yesterday, that really swanky nightclub Lombards has reopened. Why don't the three of us go there just for a giggle? We haven't been out – just us – for ages.'

'It's over twenty-ones now, isn't it?'

'What's the matter, afraid you won't get in?'

'No, I was worried about you, actually.'

She laughed. 'Anyway, they just say that to keep out the little kids. How about this Friday week?'

'Why not.'

'That'll be excellent. We'll have such a laugh, the three of us.'

'I promise I'll be in a better mood then.'

'You'd better be,' she laughed.

'Thanks for letting me rant on.'

'That's what friends are for,' she half-chanted. 'When Sophie comes round, give her a chance, and ring me tomorrow, all right.'

'I will. See you soon.'

'Take care, darlin'. Bye.'

I put the phone down and ran upstairs. I started pacing around my room. The roses on my bed in their cellophane looked all smug and glossy. They reminded me of Ryan. I flung them against the wall. They didn't look so pleased with themselves now, lying on the floor, moulting petals. Why did I buy them? What a sad person I was. I scooped them into a black bin bag. Later, after I'd eaten a very subdued meal, with neither me nor my parents saying very much, I dumped the roses in a hedge. Then I went for a long walk. I reckoned that Sophie would be calling round now. My mum would probably open the door, saying, 'Ben's not here, Sophie. He said he was going out for a walk but that was over an hour ago. I wonder where he is?' Let them wonder.

Let *her* wonder. I didn't know if I could bear to see her now anyway. All I wanted was to give her pain – and be free of her. Really, she was nothing but hassle. Look at all the grief I'd endured on her behalf: grief from the drama group, grief from my parents . . . even my friends thought less of me since I'd started seeing Sophie. Because of her, I'd diminished myself. Well, no more.

Inside my head I cried, 'Let me be free of her.' I started to walk back. I was two streets away from my house when I saw Sophie. It was starting to rain. She ran towards me. 'Here you are. Where have you been?' She sounded puzzled but there was a little smile in her voice too.

'I just felt like a walk,' I said.

Sophie looked around her. 'Oh well, nice weather for it anyway.' Then she laughed. Only it wasn't a mocking laugh: it was rather as if she was saying, 'Isn't life just absurd?' I started to laugh too. I did remind myself that I was angry with Sophie and wanted to be free of her. But my anger seemed inexplicably to have slipped away from me. And instead I was marvelling, yet again, at the way Sophie's lips curled up at the sides, and how her new bobbed hairstyle showed off her amazing jaw line.

'Have you been waiting long?' I asked.

'Yeah.' She said this with another smile. 'I had two cups of coffee round your house and then I thought I'd come and find you.'

'I'm sorry,' I said. 'I must have forgotten about the time.'

We looked at each other. 'I didn't invite Ryan round, you know,' she said. 'He was just there. I was so glad when you rang up.'

'Were you?' I asked.

'All the time Ryan was there, I was thinking I hope Ben rings up soon.'

'So what did he want?'

'Oh, he was saying a lot of rubbish,' said Sophie, 'but I wanted to talk to you about it, ask your advice.' She linked her arm in mine and we walked back to my house.

Later in my bedroom, over a glass of wine, she said, 'Ryan came round to tell me that it's all over with him and Tania.'

'Oh yeah,' I said, as casually as I could.

'They haven't actually finished but they are going to.' She looked away from me. 'He said he wants us to get back together.'

I gulped. I felt as if I'd just swallowed a stone.

'He said he's missed me so much, should never have walked out on me and I'm the girl of his dreams.' Sophie said all of this with a mocking smile, as if it was all a bit of a joke.

I picked up the theme. I gave a small cynical smile. 'He's got a nerve, hasn't he?' But inside I was shaking with frustration. Those words Ryan had used belonged to me. Sophie was the girl of my dreams. So why didn't I just steal those words back and tell Sophie what she meant to me?

Because it wasn't the right time. I didn't want her turning to me on the rebound as if I were a consolation prize. When she came to me it had to be with her whole heart.

I did feel obliged to point out Ryan's shortcomings, so I kept shaking my head as if dumbfounded by his cheek. 'I hate guys who think they can dump girls and then just pick them up again when they feel like it. But then what he probably likes is the challenge of getting you back.'

'He'll find me a big challenge then,' said Sophie.

'So what else did he say?'

127

'Not a lot,' said Sophie. 'He wants to see me to-morrow night to talk about it. He said, "just give me a hearing, that's all I ask".'

'And what did you say?'

'I said I'd have to check with you first, see if we were doing anything. Are we?'

'Not a thing . . . So do you want to see him?'

She hesitated. 'It might be amusing, see what he's going to say, then I could laugh in his face.' I smiled along with her, but I wasn't convinced. So she still hadn't got him out of her system. Maybe this next meeting would innoculate her for ever. I could wait . . . one more day.

'Just be careful he doesn't talk you into going out with him again,' I said.

'Oh, he couldn't do that,' she said.

'Don't underestimate him.'

'But these last few months have been the best of my life. And now I'm in a play. I feel as if I'm achieving so much because of you,' she gave one of her cheeky smiles, 'Sir Lancelot.'

Normally it raised my spirits to hear Sophie dub me 'Sir Lancelot'. But that time it just made me feel a bit of a fraud. I let out a small sigh. 'I'm not much of a knight you know, not really. I just play-act at it. I say a lot but I don't do anything.' I grinned sadly at her. 'Look behind my highly polished surface and you won't find much.'

Sophie put her arm around me. Her touch was always very light, more like tickling than anything else. 'Now, listen to me,' she whispered, 'I couldn't have got through these last weeks without you. I owe you so much.'

There were tears in my eyes. I started breathing hard and then I enveloped her in this massive hug which a grizzly bear might have envied. Not surprisingly, we were both a little breathless afterwards.

'I've just thought of something,' said Sophie. 'You never showed me your knight's helmet.'

'I wanted to wait until I knew you a bit better. A knight's helmet is a very intimate thing, you know. But now ...' I plunged into my wardrobe. 'I hope you're ready for this.' And so my distinctly tacky helmet was cast into the limelight once more. I tried it on. Then Sophie tried it on. And it wasn't really very funny but neither of us could stop laughing. I felt so close to her that night. Yet, all the time there was one question pounding around in my head. Finally, I asked her. 'Are you going to see Ryan tomorrow night?'

Sophie hesitated. 'No, I don't think so.' But I knew she was saying that for my sake. Really, she wanted to see him, hear the full apology.

I also knew if she didn't go, that would be all she could think about. The event would grow in her mind.

'I think you should see him,' I said.

That surprised her. 'You do?'

'Yeah, hear him out. Then you can make a decision.'

She looked at me. 'I really don't know if I want to go.'

'You go,' I said. 'And ring me when you get back, all right?'

I walked Sophie back. I wasn't home by half-past eleven but I was earlier than usual. Then I got into bed and opened *On the Road* – and a card fell out. On the envelope was written: *To Sir Lancelot*. I blinked at it in amazement, then carefully opened it.

It was a hand-made card which had on the front a picture of a jolly-looking alien, peering out of his spaceship. Then inside was written:

> *You must come from another planet*
> *to put up with me.*
> *With love,*
> *on Valentine's Day and always,*
> *Sophie XXXX*

Throughout the long day which followed, that card went everywhere with me. Even though I could recite every word on it from memory.

Finally, just after ten o'clock that night, Sophie called me.

'You're back early,' I said. 'How did it go?' I felt my throat contract as I asked.

'Oh, he had to cancel. It was a friend's eighteenth and nothing had been arranged, so it was up to Ryan to do something.'

'I see,' I said quietly.

'It is genuine, he still wants us to meet up, but he couldn't let his friend down, could he?'

I didn't argue with her but I didn't agree with her either. My undercover days as Ryan's supporter were over. Instead, I changed the subject.

'So what did you do instead?' I asked.

'Oh, I did something very exciting, I had a bath.'

'Well, now you're washed and clean, I can invite you over.'

Her voice became slightly coy. 'I'm in my nightie.'

'Even better . . . I bet you look sexy in your nightie.'

She giggled. 'Do you want to know the truth? My nightie is . . .'

'No, stop,' I interrupted. 'Don't burst my bubble.'

'Oh, sorry, I don't want to burst your bubble.'

'Just tell me this, what colour is your nightie? No, let me guess . . . It's blue. A very pale blue.'

She was amazed. 'How did you know that?'

'Because that's the colour you wear in my dreams.'

'Oh Ben,' and her voice went all muffled.

I said, 'By the way, Sophie, I was reading *On the Road* last night when out you popped. You turn up in the weirdest places, don't you?'

'I get around,' she murmured.

'Thanks for the card. I really, really like it.'

'I'm such an amazing artist, aren't I?' She was trying to sound light-hearted but it was an effort. I knew.

'You're really disappointed about Ryan not coming round, aren't you?'

'No, I'm not.'

'Don't lie to me. I am the knower of all things.'

'Well, then you'd know I'm not. Honestly.'

'All right . . . Anyway, you shouldn't be, because your life is going to be so busy, what with the play coming up and . . . Oh yes, you've got an invitation.'

'Where to?'

'To Lombards.'

'Lombards?' She sounded incredulous.

'Yeah, you know it's just reopened – well, a very exclusive group of people, namely, Jenny, Simon and myself, wondered if you'd like to join us?'

'But it's over twenty-ones, isn't it?'

'So?'

'And isn't it very expensive?'

'Amazingly, but it's all on me.'

'No, no.'

'It's my delayed but heartfelt Valentine's Day gift. So you can't turn me down.'

She let out a gasp. 'I'm stunned. I've never been to a nightclub before.'

'Not ever?'

'Not ever,' she repeated, 'and to go to Lombards . . . But what if they ask me for ID or something?'

'I'll fight them,' I said. She laughed. 'So, are you coming with us on Friday?' I asked.

'Yes, I'm going . . . thanks, Ben.' Then she gave one of her cheeky little laughs. 'I hope you enjoy your dream about me.'

'I do, every night,' I replied.

For the next few days Sophie couldn't stop talking about this trip to Lombards. Ryan was yesterday's news. I'd won all her attention. Of course, I'd had to tell a little white lie. Jenny hadn't actually invited Sophie, but I didn't see why she should mind. So I rang Jenny, and in the middle of the conversation just said, 'Sophie's really looking forward to Friday.'

'Oh, is Sophie coming as well?' asked Jenny.

'Yeah, is that OK?' I asked.

'Of course,' she replied. 'And Ryan . . . is that all . . .?'

'It's sorted,' I said, shortly.

On Friday night I put on my Cary Grant suit, and my parents raved on about how smart I looked. The atmosphere at home had been a bit strained lately, but seeing me in a suit seemed to put them in a really good mood. And when Sophie came round they proceeded to enthuse about how 'beautiful and stylish' she looked, too.

To my surprise they were right. For when she'd told me she was borrowing this long purple dress for the occasion, I feared the worst. But it was a very dark purple and gave her a real air of sophistication. My mum whispered to me, 'Sophie looks so nice, it's just a shame about her boots.'

'They're trendy, Mum, all the girls wear them here.'

Mum shook her head. 'I never thought they'd come back.'

Sophie looked cool, but she wasn't. She kept saying to me, 'Come on, test me, what's my date of birth?' And the longer we had to wait for Jenny and Simon – Jenny's dad was driving us to Lombards – the more jittery she became. In the end I rang Jenny to ask her to get a move on.

Twenty minutes later Jenny and Simon finally arrived. Jenny rushed into my house, glaring at me. 'I haven't even had time to put my hand-cream on because of you.'

She was wearing a short black skirt, black tights, and a close fitting black top. She looked stunning.

'I think the waiting was worth it,' I said. 'You look great.'

'I'm glad someone thinks so,' replied Jenny. 'Certain people keep nagging me tonight.'

'She means me, by the way, in case you were wondering,' said Simon. 'All I said was . . .'

'All he said was,' interrupted Jenny, 'that we'd need to take out a mortgage just to get in there.'

'Twenty pounds to get in, is expensive,' said Simon. 'And I was just making a joke about it.'

'Then you went on about how a bottle of Coke is five quid.'

'It is,' he said. 'But that's OK, it's worth it. Just think of all the Garys and Kevins we're going to meet tonight, passing around their single brain cell.'

'There you go,' cried Jenny. 'Look, don't do me any favours, we won't go if you like, then you can save all your precious money.'

'Oh, come on, Jenny,' I began.

'No, he's been making little digs all the way here and I hate that.'

Simon went over to her, took her hand and said, very sincerely, 'I really want to go to Lombards tonight. I was only messing about. It's worth it.'

Jenny was laughing now. 'Well, you'd better mean it, that's all . . . and, hello, Sophie, no one's talking to you –

and you look really nice.' She went over and chatted with Sophie while Simon muttered to me, 'Don't want her in a mood just before we go out, do we?'

It was half-past eleven by the time we reached Lombards. Jenny's dad said to give him a ring when we wanted to be picked up; he'd be around, no matter how late. 'He's not bad, my dad, is he?' said Jenny fondly, as we scrambled out of the car.

Sophie looked as if she were at the drama auditions again.

'You are allowed to enjoy yourself,' I murmured.

'I am enjoying myself,' protested Sophie, with a valiant smile. I squeezed her hand. Going to Lombards was a big thing for her, she'd always remember it and I'd made it happen for her.

Two shaven-headed bouncers sporting bow ties and broken noses glared down at us as we walked up the steps to the nightclub. 'Just look straight ahead,' I whispered to Sophie. They made a big thing of searching Simon and myself, but practically ignored Jenny and Sophie.

Then we were allowed to enter the glittering kingdom. 'You made it,' I whispered to Sophie.

'You can start to breathe again, Sophie,' said Jenny, quite kindly.

We handed our coats in and made our way down to the first bar. 'They've done this up,' said Jenny, admiringly. And certainly, everything gleamed and shone. But the bar was already choked up with the usual lager louts: only tonight, they were all suited up and taking themselves very seriously. Every time one of them strutted past you got a lungful of aftershave and gel was lavishly plastered over their hair. They were as self-conscious as someone at their first job interview. But they were also huntsmen in search of their quarry. They eyed Jenny and Sophie carefully. One very expensive suit leered at Jenny. 'Do those legs go all the way up?'

'That's something you'll never know,' she snapped back. 'Come on,' she said to us. 'Let's go down to the dance floor.' She nudged Sophie. 'Ben's not a bad dancer, I was really surprised. I thought he'd be rubbish.'

'Here, watch it,' I said. 'I'm an excellent mover.'

'Tell me more,' laughed Jenny.

As we walked down the steps I remember Jenny saying, 'Look at the lights on the stairs.' At that very moment Sophie slipped. She reached out for the rail and pulled herself back up, but as she did so, she let out a cry of pain. At once, I was beside her. 'Are you OK?'

Sophie was trying to laugh. 'Yeah, yeah, I just put too much weight on my foot.' I took her hand. It felt very hot. She was laughing and gasping. I knew she was in agony.

'We'll go and sit down,' I said, and Sophie, clinging

on to me, hobbled over to the tables on the edge of the dance floor. She collapsed on to a chair. 'I'm sorry,' she whispered.

'Don't be silly,' I said.

'Is it very painful?' asked Jenny.

'No, just the odd twinge,' said Sophie.

'Liar,' I replied.

There was silence for a moment then Jenny said, 'You'd need to go to training school to wear those boots.' And I know she only said that to lighten the atmosphere not as a criticism.

But immediately Sophie said, 'Look, I'll be fine just sitting here watching you three dancing . . . go on.'

'I'm not going anywhere near them,' said Simon, pointing at the only people on the dance floor, four girls going absolutely nuts.

We sat round the table and made jokes and tried to be jolly but the evening never took off and, somehow, we were back outside my house just after one o'clock.

'Are you sure you don't want me to drop you off at your house?' Jenny's dad asked Sophie.

'No, here's fine,' said Sophie. 'It's just a small sprain, that's all. Look, I'm truly sorry for ruining your night.'

'You didn't ruin it,' said Simon. 'I told you about the time I walked straight into a mirror. These things happen at nightclubs; that's what they're designed for.'

'No, don't worry about it,' said Jenny, 'there'll be other times.'

But Sophie went on: 'I'll make it up to you. Two weeks tomorrow my parents are going away for Easter and we're having a party.'

'What, you and Nick?' I exclaimed.

'Yes, I know wonders will never cease,' she laughed.

'I didn't know about this,' I said.

'I only knew myself tonight,' replied Sophie. 'But you both must come,' she turned to Jenny's dad, 'and you too.'

He chuckled. 'Thanks, Sophie, but I think I'll take a raincheck on that one.'

I helped Sophie out of the car and upstairs to my room. I made her a very sweet cup of tea, which she drank whilst lounging back on my bed.

'It wasn't really my boots,' she announced, suddenly. 'You know Jenny said . . .'

'She didn't mean anything by that.'

'I know, but it wasn't my boots. I've worn them loads of times. It's only, tonight I was looking all around me when, wham, I just lost my balance. Jenny's really cross with me, isn't she?'

'Not at all. Anyone can fall over at any age.'

'Ben, I am . . .'

'You're not going to apologise again, are you?'

She half-smiled. 'Yes.'

'Well, don't, please.'

'But you didn't even dance tonight and Jenny said you were a good dancer.'

'That's rubbish,' I replied. 'Do you want to know the real truth? I loathe dancing at nightclubs.'

'Do you?' Sophie looked shocked.

'The last time I danced at a nightclub,' I started to laugh, 'I looked down and suddenly realised I hadn't done anything with my feet for about ten hours, so I started shifting my feet around and I didn't know what I was doing.' I laughed again. 'And all the time I was trying to wear this very serious expression, like "I'm really into this music".'

Sophie was starting to laugh now, so I swept on: 'I tell you, at the end of an evening at a nightclub you come away exhausted, not because you've been dancing all night, but because you couldn't pretend to enjoy it another minute. So then you leave at four in the morning with no money, bloodshot eyes, a splitting headache for about two weeks and some daft tune going round and round in your head. But at least you've been there and there's only one thing worse than going to a nightclub and that's feeling you've missed out.'

I stopped for breath. Sophie started clapping, grinning broadly. 'You're funny,' she said.

'I'll take that as a compliment,' I said.

'Oh, yes,' she cried. 'I like the way you look at things, because you see things as they are and that helps me.'

'Want to know the truth about something else?' I said. 'You carried it off tonight really well. I was proud of you.'

'Were you really?'

'I said so, didn't I?'

'Say it again.' She pressed herself tightly against me.

'I'll tell you something else. Ernie's really pleased with you.'

'He never says anything at rehearsals.'

'That's not his style but I can tell. You're just doing so much.'

'Yes, I am, aren't I? All the girls in my year are so jealous.'

'So you tell them what you get up to, do you?'

'Do you mind?'

'No, not at all. And what about your family?'

She shrugged her shoulders. 'I tell them bits,' she said, 'but I can't talk to them. Nothing's real in our house. My parents spend their whole life pretending. Like this trip at Easter. I know why they're doing it. They didn't tell me the real reason. But I know. You see, about two years ago, my dad walked out. He'd met this other woman. I was away on a trip to Swanage and by the time

I came back he was home again. My mum goes, "Your dad has got something to say to you," and he was sitting in his chair, telling me he'd been very naughty. Then we never mentioned it again, until . . . I was at a New Year's Eve party and my mum rang me up. "He's gone again," she said. This time he was away much longer. And I really didn't think my mum would have him back.' She gave a wry smile. 'But she did, right away.

'Now my dad spends all his time in the greenhouse with his portable phone. And I'm sure he's ringing one of his women friends. There's something going on, and this Easter trip is to try and sort things out. They're always trying to sort things out, but they never do. They just tiptoe round each other, pretending. They make me sick sometimes.'

There was a beat of silence.

Then I said, quietly, 'Just remember, whatever happens, you've always got Sir Lancelot. He'll never let you down. Never.'

Suddenly, she raised her head and we were staring into each other's eyes. I don't remember how long we held that look. I just remember this great wave of elation.

I wanted to give her everything. And the more I gave her the more I discovered inside myself. Life was looking so good. But there was still one shadow on the X-ray. RYAN.

He was still ringing Sophie with his phoney little dilemma: his boss, according to Ryan, was making advances towards him again. While he just wanted to get back with Sophie. Sophie was much more sceptical of him now, but he still bothered her. He bothered me too, especially when he'd ask Sophie to pass on some putrid message to me, like: 'Ryan sends you his best' and 'Ryan says, good luck with the play'.

I had a message for him too: Ryan, get stuffed.

Sophie thought he was just trying to be nice. But I knew what he was really saying: 'You're no threat to me. When the time comes, I can take Sophie away from you very easily.'

Maybe he was right. I had to know. I didn't have long to wait. The showdown happened at Sophie's party.

2 . . . Showdown with Ryan

Why did I dread that party so much? Maybe it was just that I felt totally excluded from the whole event. I wasn't involved in the planning of it at all. And now Ryan was going to be there. That was the real bombshell.

'What's he coming for?' I demanded, when Sophie told me the day before the party.

'Well, he just sort of invited himself,' she said.

'But how did he know about it?'

'I don't know, really.' Sophie was annoyingly vague. 'He just heard about it.'

We were in my bedroom. I got up, blew out the candle and put my harsh, artificial light on.

'What did you do that for?' asked Sophie.

'Oh, what's the point,' I said, wearily. 'What's the

point of anything? If he turns up tomorrow it will just cause more grief and aggro for everyone, especially you,' I added, angry now.

'But what else can I do?' demanded Sophie. 'I can't tell him not to come.'

'Why?'

'I can't just turn my back on him.'

'But he's turned his back on you.'

'No, he hasn't,' she said quietly.

'Well, he dumped you.'

She reddened. That had caught her. At once, I stopped. I sat down on the bed next to her.

'He probably won't even turn up,' said Sophie, staring down at the carpet. 'I really hope he doesn't.' I didn't answer.

For once, she left early. Just mentioning him was poisoning the atmosphere between us now. I felt lonely and scared.

I rang up Simon and persuaded him and Jenny to come to the party.

They arrived at my house for seven o'clock. Jenny went into the kitchen to have a chat with my mum, while Simon, Dad and myself discussed the perilous state of British cricket. Normally I hated staying in on a Saturday night. But tonight I felt so relaxed and secure, I didn't want to leave. But then I thought of Ryan prowling around, giving Sophie another sob story. I had to be there.

My dad was in such a good mood he drove us to Sophie's. There were balloons hanging from the windows and chart-hits could be heard pounding down the road. And for the first time that day it wasn't raining. I was disappointed – I'd quite liked the idea of arriving in the middle of a thunderstorm.

We hovered on the doorstep.

'Well, go on, ring the doorbell,' said Jenny. 'You're getting me all nervous now.'

I whirled round. 'If Ryan's there, giving me one of his cheesy smiles . . .'

'Just remember,' said Simon, patting me on the back, 'you've got your henchmen right behind you.'

I rang the doorbell. There were some scuffling noises and through the glass door I could see blurred shapes rushing past. The door was pushed open with some difficulty. Sophie popped her head around the door, grinning. 'Hang on, one of the trainers has got wedged under the door, there we go . . .' She was dressed very casually but she was wearing some quite flash earrings which Jenny instantly admired.

She greeted us warmly. 'I was hoping you'd get here soon. Come in, ignore all the dirty shoes. It's been chaos here. Luckily everyone's kept quiet about it, so we haven't had any gatecrashers.' Sophie grinned at us again;

she seemed very high tonight. Several people passed us in the hallway. Sophie introduced us to a couple of them – girls from her form who stared at us curiously – and then we saw Nick coming down the stairs. He saw me and his face lit up. 'Well, if it isn't Carruthers.'

I was pleased to see him too. Yet 'Carruthers' seemed to belong to another age. It was like hearing a nickname from middle school. We grinned rather desperately at each other. We both still liked one another, but we didn't really have anything to say any more.

'It's buzzing in here, isn't it?' said Simon.

'Yes, it's great,' I agreed. I introduced Nick to Simon and Jenny. He greeted them warmly and then we had another faltering conversation. Finally, Sophie ushered us into the kitchen to get a drink.

Wedged round the pine table in the corner were a group of lads I recognised from the sports centre. I nodded to them and some of them waved at me. Cans of beer were stacked up in front of them like a line of defence. And every so often the table would rock with laughter. Otherwise, the kitchen was full of people who seemed endlessly on the move. I spotted Vanessa. 'We wondered when you'd be coming,' she said. 'I think Sophie was getting anxious.'

'Was she really?' I said. Sophie was now helping Simon and Jenny to drinks.

Vanessa looked at me for a moment. 'I hear the rehearsals for the play are going well.'

'Yeah, not bad, you'll have to come along to the competition. We've got some tickets for . . . friends and supporters.'

'I might just do that,' laughed Vanessa to my relief. Suddenly, she darted past me with an ashtray. 'Do you mind,' she said, to this rather startled-looking guy. 'It's just, ash is messy and it smells, as well.' She leapt back to me.

'You'll be handing out beer mats next,' I said.

'Now, there's an idea,' she smiled. 'Did Nick tell you I'd moved in?'

'No he didn't.'

'Well, I have. I just couldn't stand it in my house any more. Yesterday my beloved stepdad had another go at me about university. He said if I don't go I'm letting my mother down – and him. I said it was nothing to do with him, and it isn't. But then my mum started on me, saying how I wasn't giving him a chance and he was only trying to help. She always takes his side. So I thought, that's it, I'm out of here and Sophie said I could share with her, not that there's room for even one person in her room. Still, I don't care where I sleep, anything to get out of there.'

Simon and Jenny came over and we chatted quite

amiably until the doorbell rang again and this girl rushed into the kitchen. 'Vanessa, it's the man from next door again.'

'Oh hell, I'd better speak to him,' said Vanessa, rushing off.

'She's all right, really,' said Jenny, nodding after Vanessa. 'I hated her at school, but she's improved.' Then Jenny nudged me. The table appeared to be speaking.

'It's Jenny, isn't it? I'd know those legs anywhere.' Then the voice added, 'I'm down here.' And sitting under the table, right in the corner, was a heavily-bearded guy in an old army jacket.

'Oh, hello, Bob,' cried Jenny. 'What are you doing down there?'

'It's good down here,' he said. 'No one bothers you and you see what's going on. Come down and have a chat.'

Jenny giggled. 'OK,' she said. 'Are you two coming down as well?'

'No, we couldn't stand the excitement,' said Simon. 'But you enjoy yourself.' Then he turned to me. 'No sign of Ryan the rat, then.'

'Don't rejoice too soon,' I replied. I looked around me. Out of the corner of my eye I could see Sophie darting about. I know she had to circulate, but she'd hardly spoken to me. No wonder I felt so distant from her tonight; almost as if I'd lost my special role in her life. I began to feel edgy and resentful.

And then Ryan arrived. He was wearing a baseball cap, blue sports vest, black jeans and boots. He might have looked OK in Los Angeles, but here he just looked like a total stiff. He came over to me grinning, hand outstretched. I nailed a smile on to my face.

'Hi, good to see you again,' he said. I introduced him to Simon, who smiled bleakly at him, while Sophie hovered uncertainly. Finally, Ryan said he'd better go and say hello to Vanessa and disappeared into the lounge. Shortly afterwards Sophie disappeared too. Ryan was certainly receiving more attention from her than she gave me.

Then the two girls from her class started up. 'Ryan's really nice, isn't he?'

'Yeah, Sophie's so lucky to have him.'

I couldn't listen to any more of that gush. I blundered past them and out into the back garden. The grass was soaking wet. I took some deep breaths, then looked around and saw Simon standing beside me.

He gave me one of his hesitant smiles. I suddenly realised both my hands were clenched into fists.

'I've had it with this, Simon . . . I have. What did you think of him?'

'He's just so corny,' began Simon.

'Exactly. It's obvious what he is. So what is she think-ing about, having him here? I'm wasting my time, aren't I?'

'I think you're getting carried away too quickly,' said Simon.

'But do you blame me, with that Ryan smirking about the place. I tell you, I'm going to swing for him.'

'Look, I think we should go and chill out somewhere then we can talk about this. Plan a strategy.'

'But if I leave, Ryan's won,' I said.

'No, he hasn't,' said Simon firmly. 'If you go, he doesn't know anything, he can only speculate. But if he sees you sobbing on the grass, then he's won. Don't open up here.'

'All right,' I said. 'We'll go. But first I want to see Sophie and tell her . . .' What did I want to tell her? I felt suddenly giddy with pain. 'Just tell her,' I said.

I marched back into the kitchen. It was much emptier now, though the lads were still in residence and from under the table came Jenny's throaty laugh.

'Jenny, we're going,' muttered Simon.

At once she popped up. 'See you then, Bob,' she cried. 'He's so funny, has me in stitches. Why are we going so early?' Then she saw my face. 'OK, I get it.'

'I just want to say goodbye to Sophie,' I said.

'She'll probably be in the lounge,' said Jenny. 'It's all happening in there.'

And the lounge was now one huge mass of thumping feet. Everyone was dancing. I pushed through the crowd. I spotted Vanessa looking around her anxiously, but there was no sign of Sophie.

'Where the hell is she?' I cried. 'I'm sick of looking for her . . . I spend my life looking for her.'

'She's around,' murmured Jenny. 'We'll find her.' She turned to a girl. 'You haven't seen Sophie anywhere, have you?'

'Yes. She was with Ryan . . .' She raised her eyebrows. 'They went upstairs.'

I stormed my way out of the lounge with Jenny and Simon close behind me.

'Now, I know what you're thinking,' said Jenny.

'Do you?' I cried.

'Yes, and you mustn't jump to conclusions.'

'Look, let's just split,' said Simon.

But already, I was walking up the stairs.

'Ben, what are you doing?' Jenny called, in a piercing whisper after me.

I didn't answer her. I just went on up the stairs. I heard Jenny call me again. But something pushed me on. I couldn't stop now. I remembered where her room was. The door was slightly ajar. It was in darkness. And it was empty.

I peeked into Nick's room. That was empty as well.

So she must have gone into her parents' bedroom. For a wild instant I wanted to storm in there. But I didn't. Instead, I returned to Sophie's room. I don't exactly know why. I stood there, listening to the rain blowing against her window. A strange mournful sound. A strange room, too. Once again the smallness of it hit me. I sat on the edge of the bed. The last time I was in here I was comforting her after Ryan had walked out. Ever since, I'd devoted my life to her. And what was my reward: Sophie rolling about on her parents' double bed with him.

A couple of nights ago I'd been lying on the sofa at home kissing her. And afterwards she said to me, 'You kissed me six times.' As if kissing was still a thing she counted, as if each kiss meant something. I really liked the way she said that. And also, how, when I was kissing her she kept on moving her hands about, as if she didn't quite know what to do with them. And then finally, daringly, she wrapped her arms around me. Her freshness and inexperience charmed me. And I respected it. One day in the future, she and I would make love. I'd often imagined the scene: she and I would lie together in front of a large open fire that was blazing away. And I'd be gentle and kind – and we'd both be so full of love . . .

Only, it was Ryan she wanted to play that scene with. Shallow, manipulative, laddish Ryan. I jumped up. It was so claustrophobic in here. I rushed back downstairs; Jenny and Simon were waiting, grim-faced.

I looked at them, then looked upstairs. 'Bye then,' I shouted. 'We're going now. Bye! Bye!' I stopped, breathless. The door opened as silently as the door in a dream. And there was Sophie, standing at the top of the stairs, gazing down at us. The landing light gave her a ghostly aura.

'Where are you going? What's wrong?' she asked.

'We didn't think you'd notice if we left,' I cried. I felt Jenny nudge me not to say any more. But it was too late. The words leapt out of me. 'You've got Ryan and that's all you want, isn't it? So we're going.'

She stared down, her face pale and anxious. 'No, wait,' she said. She half-ran down those stairs. Then on the bottom step, she said, softly, 'I don't want you to go.'

'Well, you've got a strange way of showing it,' I cried. 'Up there with him.'

'He's upset.'

I turned away, then cried, 'But what about me?'

'I've been trying to tell him that we can't go on like this,' said Sophie. 'I wanted to be his friend and help him but . . . it's just not working. I can't have this any more. It's over between us and what he does with his boss is up to him alone. That's what I was explaining to him when you called me.'

'Really,' I said, disbelievingly.

'And all the time I was with him I could hear you and Jenny and Simon talking downstairs and I longed to be down here with you. You've got to believe that.'

Upstairs the door opened noiselessly again. Ryan was standing at the top of the stairs now. And for once he wasn't smiling. He stared down at me; as nasty a look as I'd ever seen. Then he started walking down the stairs. Sophie edged closer to me. On the bottom step he paused, just for a moment. I had my right arm around Sophie now. I thought he was going to say something, but he just gave us this grim, little smile before sauntering out of the door. I looked at Sophie. Her face was blank, expressionless. Then the kitchen door opened and this girl was bleating, 'Sophie, some glasses have been broken. Do you want to have a look?'

Sophie stared about her as if she didn't know where she was. 'Yeah, OK. I'll be back,' she whispered to me. She went into the kitchen, Jenny followed her. Simon half-grinned at me.

'It had to be done,' I said, at last. 'I couldn't let Sophie be messed about like that.'

He nodded, then said, 'The look he gave you. Talk about a death stare . . .'

I felt as if I'd received a medal. At last, Ryan realised I wasn't to be messed with. I'd been elevated into an enemy. Shortly afterwards Jenny reappeared. She looked really shaken. 'Are you OK?' I asked.

'Oh, I'm fine,' she said sarcastically, 'hearing you shouting at Sophie like that. We didn't know what was going to happen.'

'Come on, it was worth it to see Ryan getting what he deserved,' grinned Simon.

But Jenny shook her head. 'I was really worried that the others would start listening. I just wanted everything to calm down.'

'It had to be done,' I repeated flatly.

'But this wasn't the right place,' she said.

But then Sophie was by my side. 'Everything all right in there?' I asked.

'Sort of, I'll worry about all that tomorrow. Do you fancy some fresh air?'

'Yeah, definitely.'

Sophie and I went out of the front door. She closed the door behind her and we carried on walking.

'Are we going anywhere in particular?' I asked.

'Who knows?' She smiled at me.

'When Ryan left . . .' I began.

'He's gone,' she said simply.

But I still wasn't satisfied. 'So you've no regrets about him?' The rain had eased off, although it was still very windy; the air felt suddenly fresh.

Then Sophie said, in a voice so soft I could hardly hear it above the wind, 'I thought you were going to walk out on me.'

I stopped and gazed at her. 'I'll never leave you,' I whispered, only the wind seemed to carry my words away, so I almost shouted, 'Never.' She was smiling at me now in that open, fragile way of hers. Then she hooked her arm into mine.

1 . . . Preview of Heaven

The next ten weeks and four days were the happiest of my life. The only thing is, it's hard to recall exactly what happened when all the memories seem to run into each other now. So many good memories; but then, I saw Sophie every day.

We did try and mark off time to revise for exams. I remember we said we wouldn't meet up one evening, as I had an exam the next day. But then, just after eight o'clock Sophie called me. And she asked me how it was all going, then she said, 'Do you want me to come round and test you or anything?' Of course, I said, 'Yes,' (even though it wasn't the kind of exam you can test people on) and then I realised that here she was, my dream-girl, and she couldn't spend enough time with me. As for the exams: I floated through them as if I'd been anaes-thetised. Even when I was turning over my paper I was singing inside my head. For I knew, whatever happened, I had a prize beyond any other.

On the Tuesday after her party I sent Sophie twelve red roses and on the card I wrote: *With all my love, Sir Lancelot*. I wanted to get her a present as well. She said, 'No, you've done enough already.' But I insisted. She said she'd let me know what she wanted. And the following day I got this single red rose and on the card was written: *Send me your pillow, the one you dream on, and I'll send you mine*. At first I thought she'd made those lines up herself, but then I discovered she'd 'borrowed' them from Morrissey. I'll keep that card until the day I die. And I sent her one of my pillows. It sounds so silly and corny now. Yet, something had happened, deep inside ourselves and it had to be expressed.

Sophie seemed such a long way from the deathly pale figure I'd known in January. I became closer to her than I'd ever been to anyone, even Simon and Jenny. It was so exhilarating. The way I saw it, I was building a skyscraper and each time I saw Sophie it was as if I were putting down another floor until one day, I'd be as close to heaven as it was possible to be.

A preview of heaven – that's how I'd sum up those weeks. For the first time I quite liked myself too. I was

159

more than I thought I was. There were so many high-lights of those weeks. But if I had to choose just one, I know what it would be.

I'd been invited to the end-of-year sixth-form party. It was going to be quite a lavish affair, and it was free, so I was quite keen to go. Most of the sixth form were taking partners with them: of course, I invited Sophie.

'I'd rather not,' she said.

'Oh, come on,' I urged.

'No, I don't think I could face it.'

'Why?'

'I'd just feel awkward there,' she said. 'I wouldn't enjoy it.'

I didn't push it any more. But I was very disappointed. And there was just a slight coolness between us when we parted that night. I went to the party on my own and didn't have a good time at all. It was as if I were just an onlooker, wandering around, observing. I chatted to people, and exchanged phone numbers and promised to keep in touch, but they were empty conversations and that was my fault: I didn't feel as if I had anything inter-esting to say. I gazed idly around me and then, to my astonishment, I saw her standing by the door chatting to Laura from the drama group, looking amazingly poised in a blue and white top I'd never seen before. She saw me, smiled mischievously, then carried on talking to Laura.

I felt strangely shy when I first spoke to her. 'So you're here after all.'

'Yeah, well, there was nothing on television, so I thought I might as well turn up,' she pointed to her blue and white stripes, 'cunningly disguised as a deckchair.'

'I'm so . . .' I began, then shrugged my shoulders and smiled. I was practically speechless.

Sophie took my arm. 'Come on, Sir Lancelot, I want one of those free drinks,' she said, and gave me one of her sudden, dazzling smiles. It was as if we were having a reconciliation without having to go through all the hassle of quarrelling. I was absurdly happy.

And I couldn't get over how relaxed and confident Sophie seemed that night. But then she never stopped surprising me: she had so many colours. Later she told me, 'I was incredibly nervous about that party but I knew if I didn't go I'd be letting you down. So what I did, was, I imagined I was in a play, acting the role of this very sophisticated character. Over and over I rehearsed how I'd come in, what I'd say . . .'

'Ernie would have been proud of you,' I replied.

Ernie was quite impressed with Sophie, anyway. She worked hard at rehearsals and she was genuinely interested in Ernie's theories about acting. She'd say, 'Ernie told me today, if my attitude to the character is right, however I say my lines cannot be wrong.'

So together we'd work out Sophie's attitude to her character. And at night we'd watch lots of very old films, so Sophie could pick up the atmosphere. But it wasn't until the night of the competition that I realised how good she was.

I was in my old man's costume telling my grand-daughter and her fiancé about the only girl I ever loved. Then I put on the video. And there was Sophie. You only saw her fleetingly, but the audience responded to her at once, especially the way she said her last line: 'I'll be waiting . . . I'll wait for ever, for you.' Ernie had been worried she'd said it too softly, but there was a hushed silence in the theatre, followed by a little rustle of 'Who was that?' I really believe a star was born that night. I can't tell you how proud I felt. Winning the competition was almost an anticlimax. Still, it was pretty exciting to win. Especially as it meant we'd be performing the play again, all expenses paid (Sophie as well, even though she had already recorded her part) at the Edinburgh Festival in August.

And then came more exciting news. The director of a touring company had seen my play and wanted to com-mission me to write another one: a thirty-minute play about bullying in schools. When I told Sophie she was ecstatic. 'I'm just so happy for you,' she said, over and over. In fact, she said it so often I started laughing at her.

Then she became indignant. 'Stop laughing at me. You really don't know how much I care about you.'

Those were her exact words. Three days later, she walked out on me. And I still don't know why. Everything was going so well. We didn't have any arguments. There was no tension between us. Yet, there must have been some hint in those days. Somewhere, I must be able to find the beginnings of the catastrophe. I knew Sophie had had a couple of bad migraines and she was going to get some tablets, but that was nothing to do with me. What else? Well, relations had become strained between Sophie and Jenny.

One day Sophie said to me, 'I don't think Jenny likes me very much, does she?'

'Of course she does,' I replied. 'What makes you say that?'

'I don't know, just a feeling and . . .' she hesitated.

'Go on,' I said.

'If I tell you this, do you promise not to tell Jenny?'

'Yeah, OK,' I began.

'No, you must promise.' Suddenly, she was very grave.

'All right, I promise,' I said.

'You know at my party when Ryan left?'

I winced slightly. We hardly ever mentioned Ryan now.

'Well, I went into the kitchen to see what had been broken and Jenny followed me, and she said, "If you want to go off with Ryan, we will support you." '

I stared at her dubiously. 'Jenny said that?'

'And she went on about it and I thought, she wants me out of everything, that's why she's pushing me back to Ryan.'

'No, Jenny wouldn't do that,' I argued, but it was a very half-hearted defence. I couldn't help remembering how strange Jenny had been afterwards. And she hadn't seemed at all pleased I'd seen Ryan off.

I kept my promise to Sophie. I didn't say anything to Jenny. Instead, I discussed it, in strictest confidence, with Simon. He, typically, underplayed the whole thing. 'Jenny's never said anything to me against Sophie. She likes her.' He paused but then just said, again, 'No, she likes Sophie.'

Yet I had a feeling he was keeping something back. Now Simon had his secrets and I had mine. I didn't really like that. So when I heard about my new commission I thought it would be a good chance for the four of us to get together and celebrate.

And that brings us to the dreaded day: Friday, 22 July. The night of celebration that ended in disaster. My mum, dad and Glen were away at my Aunt Annie's. Earlier, my dad had rung me to say there was a bottle of champagne in the fridge, and he wanted me to open that and toast the play with my friends. So we opened the champagne. But it wasn't as great as we'd hoped: it was slightly flat, actually.

Like the evening itself.

I remember putting a video on and then some CDs, but everyone seemed very restless. Later, Simon and Jenny watched this music programme, while Sophie and I chatted on the stairs. At first we had quite a light, flirtatious conversation. She was wearing a top I'd never seen before. I said she looked really nice in it, I told her that I really needed her help with the play about bullying. I suggested we work on the plot together . . . easy, harmless stuff. Then I said to her that my parents were away so she could stay as long as she liked.

'I don't think I'd better.' Sophie smiled apologetic-ally. 'My parents wouldn't like it.'

'Your parents,' I echoed disbelievingly.

'Yeah, they've started having a go at me about this and that . . . they're worried about me.'

'What are they worried about?' I demanded.

'Oh, lots of things: what's going to become of me now I've finished my GCSEs.'

'But haven't you told them all the things you've been doing? I mean, you're really taking off, don't they see that?'

Again, she gave me that apologetic smile. 'I don't think it's real to them.'

I was getting more and more irritated. 'They're good ones to talk.'

'They want me home more, and don't want me staying out so late at night. They think I should slow things down a bit.' She shrugged her shoulders. 'I suppose I'd better do what they want.'

'Why, you've achieved more things here than they can dream about in their narrow little world. Tomorrow we're starting to write a play that will be performed in schools around the country.'

'I know, and that's good.' But there was something forced in the way she said it. Suddenly, inexplicably, she was slipping away from me. I was angry and afraid.

All at once I was shouting at her. 'What you're saying is very insulting to me. I do all this for you and you just let your parents brush it all away.'

'No I'm not.'

'What are you saying, then?'

'I'm just saying I've got to take note of what they think.'

'But they've done nothing for you. I'm the one who's . . . I don't believe you.'

She sat on the stairs staring at me, not saying anything.

'Well, thanks a lot, you're just like all my other girl-friends; they were disappointing and so are you.' I should have apologised there and then. In a far outpost of my mind I knew that. But instead, I saw her eyes fill up with pain and I drank in that sight. And then there was no time to say anything else. Jenny was in the doorway, saying, 'What are you two doing out here?'

We gave Jenny pinched little smiles and followed her into the lounge. The music programme was still blaring away. Sophie stood staring at the screen, but her eyes seemed far away. I would have to apologise to her. But I went into the kitchen to make tea and then I heard the front door slam. I ran into the lounge and stared around me.

'Was that Sophie?' I asked.

'Yeah, she just said she had to go,' began Jenny.

I raced out of the front door. Sophie was only a few metres in front of me.

'Sophie,' I cried.

But she didn't turn round, she just kept on walking.

'Sophie, Sophie,' I yelled. 'Wait, please.'

And then suddenly she did turn round. 'I'm sorry I'm a disappointment to you.'

I stared at her, feeling full of guilt and anguish. But already she was walking away from me again. 'Sophie, listen, you must listen.' I ran around in front of her.

'What I said was so stupid and pathetic and it wasn't true.'

But she wouldn't look at me. She didn't appear to be even listening.

'Sophie, don't go like this, please.' I reached out to touch her.

'No,' she shrieked. 'No.'

I immediately fell back. She started running. I ran behind her, calling out, 'Sophie, at least let me apologise, at least let me do that. I'm sorry, what more can I say? Sophie, I beg you, don't go like this.' My words echoed down the dark, deserted road. But none of the words reached her. She just carried on running, faster and faster away from me. Finally, I cried, 'All right, go then, if you want to be stupid! Go.'

I walked quickly back, bristling with righteous indignation. She never even gave me a chance to explain. She'd gone way over the top. And soon she'd see that and be ashamed of herself. No point in telling Simon and Jenny anything. Tomorrow, Sophie and I would be laughing about this, after Sophie had apologised to me. But I wouldn't make a big thing about it. I'd just quietly say we should never run out on each other. We deserved better than that.

Simon and Jenny were waiting by the door. 'Is everything OK?' asked Jenny, anxiously.

I tried to look carefree and amused. 'Everything's fine,' I said. 'Sophie just had one of her headaches. I think they're beginning to get her down. She said goodnight and hopes to see you soon.'

But neither Simon nor Jenny looked very convinced.

'Was it something I said?' asked Jenny. 'It was, wasn't it?'

'No, don't be silly, it was just a bad migraine.'

Shortly afterwards Jenny and Simon got a taxi home, while I lay in bed, going over and over the argument in my mind. If only I hadn't said it. Sophie had never disappointed me. Why couldn't she just turn round and say, 'That's OK, I know you didn't mean it,' or even have a go at me: 'Don't ever say that to me again.' I'd much rather she told me off than just run away. She was the one who'd turned this into a major drama.

I finally fell asleep at about four o'clock and woke up again three hours later. As I made myself tea and toast, the events of last night seemed far away, a bad dream. Sophie and I would sort out this situation in about twenty seconds. I'd say, 'I'm sorry,' she'd say, 'No, I'm sorry,' and we'd fall into each other's arms; crisis over.

Greatly comforted by this scenario, I sat and watched breakfast television. Sophie was due around my house at about eleven that morning to start working on the play so I decided not to ring her. But Sophie didn't turn up at eleven or five past or ten past . . . At half-past eleven I rang her house. No answer. I was becoming agitated now. It was so weird, no one answering. So I sprinted round to Sophie's house. It was bucketing down with rain, but I hardly noticed. I rang the bell twice. There was no reply. The house was dead. I stood outside in the rain, waiting. Finally, I took shelter in a phone box down the road. The windows were all misted up and it was difficult to see out. But every time a figure rushed past I jumped out of the telephone box just in case it was Sophie. Then I started ringing up her house. I knew there was no one in but, for some obscure reason, I still kept on phoning.

At last I rang Simon. I told him I only had ten pence left and would he ring me back.

'Where are you?' he asked.

'In a phone box.'

'I know that. But where?'

'Down Sophie's road.' It was such a relief to tell some-one else what happened. At the end he said slowly, 'All right, Sophie's stormed off . . . girls often do that. It's just a gesture to show you've hurt them.'

'I have apologised . . .'

'Yeah, but she wants to make you suffer a bit more.'

'She's doing that all right.'

'It's all part of the game,' said Simon. 'Like, you remember Vicky.'

'Yeah.' Simon had gone out with Vicky two or three years ago.

'Well, she was always storming off,' said Simon. 'But it never lasted more than twenty-four hours, did it?'

'No, that's true,' I remembered.

'It's like a kind of twenty-four-hour sickness,' said Simon. 'You mustn't rush them. I'd wait now until tomorrow.'

Tomorrow seemed decades away.

'Yeah, she needs a bit of time,' said Simon. 'But she'll be back. She likes you and, basically, she's a really nice girl.'

'I know, that's why this is so out of character.' My voice began to shake. 'I can't lose her, Simon.'

'You're not going to lose her,' said Simon, reassuringly. 'Just give her time to get over it. Personally, I'd abandon the stake-out in the phone box. Why don't I come round to your house, or you come round to mine?'

'I think I'd like to come round to you,' I said. 'I'm sick of being in my house.'

'Excellent. Come round and we'll do something exciting, like . . . well, I'll think of something.' Then he added, 'I really would leave it for today, though.'

In moments of crisis, Simon came up trumps every time. But as soon as I got home to change before going to Simon's all I could do was stare at the phone. I couldn't

171

wait. I rang and rang and finally, at half-past four, the phone was picked up by Vanessa.

At last, human contact. 'Hi, Vanessa, it's Ben.'

'I know, I recognised your voice,' she said. She was warm, friendly, even slightly flirty.

'Is Sophie there, please?'

'Yeah, she's just come in. I'll get her for you.'

Everything felt normal again. But then Vanessa was back on the line. 'I'm sorry, Ben, she won't come to the phone.' She sounded puzzled and confused.

'Oh no,' I cried.

'What's happened?' asked Vanessa.

'I said something I shouldn't, something very stupid. But I didn't mean it and I've just been trying to apologise . . . please get her to the phone, please, please.'

'Yes, all right, Ben.' Vanessa's tone was pacifying. 'Just wait there, I'll get her.'

I stood trembling. I shouldn't have gushed on to Vanessa like that – I was practically crying on the phone. And maybe Nick was there too, listening. But, if it brought Sophie to the phone I didn't care.

And then I heard Sophie say, 'Hello,' in a very low, flat voice.

'Sophie,' I began. 'I wanted to apologise to you about . . .'

'I'm sorry I'm such a disappointment to you.' Her

words rushed over mine and there was so much anguish and pain in them, my heart turned over.

'Sophie, you're not a disappointment to me. I never meant that . . .'

'And I won't have you saying things about my family,' she cried, her voice shaking with emotion.

'I didn't say anything about . . .' But then I stopped. There was no point in saying any more. The phone had gone dead. I stared at it disbelievingly. I'd said one stupid thing to Sophie and she wouldn't let me apologise for it. But what I'd said meant nothing. Surely she knew that. How was I to sort this out? I should be round at Simon's. I should leave it for now. Instead, I pounded back to Sophie's house and rang the bell. Vanessa opened the door.

'Hi, Ben,' she said, in a tone which suggested she knew why I was here, and didn't fancy my chances.

'Please get her to talk to me, Vanessa. I know we can sort this out, if only she'll give me a chance. She owes me that, at least, doesn't she?'

Vanessa nodded gravely, but then said, 'Wait here,' and left me standing on the step. Normally I'd have been invited in but today, I'd fallen from glory. Waiting outside was a small humiliation, but I felt it keenly.

Vanessa was gone for ages. Was this a good sign? I kept looking for hopeful signs. The sun was coming out and I thought maybe this was a good omen. But then Vanessa returned. 'I'm sorry, Ben, she refuses to see you.'

'This is so stupid,' I cried. 'It's all getting blown up into something it's not. I said one stupid, hateful thing, and I shouldn't have done, but I've also said lots of very good, positive things to Sophie. Yet all this is wiped out by one little mistake. I mean, she's taken this out of all proportion.'

'Maybe,' said Vanessa. 'But she is upset and . . . look, the best thing you can do, Ben, is leave it a while. She'll come round, just give her some time.'

I raised my hand in frustration. 'But if she'd just see me, I know I could sort this out. There's nothing to sort out really.'

'Maybe it's not just what you said.' Vanessa lowered her voice confidingly. 'Things have been a bit strained here lately . . . Still, Nick and I are going away next week.'

'Where?'

'We're going to stay with my dad in Devon. When he heard how badly I'd been treated by Mum and her man, he invited Nick and me to stay with him for as long as we wanted.' She said this proudly. 'He said it wasn't right that I was pushed out of my house just because I didn't want to go to university.'

'I'm sure you'll have a good time,' I said.

'I'm looking forward to it . . . I'll have another word with Sophie.'

'Thanks, Vanessa.'

'Just give her a chance to cool down.'

Then I went round Simon's and we spent half the night going over what happened. I'd disregarded Simon's earlier advice which made me feel rather sheepish but he just moved on to the next stage of the crisis.

'All you can do now is play the waiting game. It's hard, but it's all you can do.'

'So you definitely don't think I should ring or go round again?'

'No,' replied Simon, firmly. 'She knows how you feel. It's up to her now.'

I agreed with him until I got home. It was after two o'clock in the morning now, so I knew I couldn't ring. But I had to do something so I set off for Windmill Hill with my writing pad and wrote Sophie a letter. Correction. I wrote her several letters.

Here is the one I sent her:

Dear Sophie,

I'm sitting on the top of Windmill Hill. It's a warm night, with just a hint of a breeze. And the sky is full of small stars. If I were here with you, I'd say it was a beautiful night. But without you, nothing reaches me.

Do you know, I keep looking for you here. I even fancied that when I reached the top you'd be waiting for me, and I'd take you in my arms and hold you so tight and whisper to you to forgive me.

What I said last Friday, and it doesn't bear repeating, was said in a burst of ego. I was angry and upset, because I didn't think you were appreciating me. Pitiful, isn't it? So I wanted to wound you, because I was burning up with frustration. But I am truly sorry. I knew as soon as I'd said it, that I was wrong.

Once you told me that I was the only person you ever listened to. Remember? And I was so honoured when you said that. Please listen to me now. That silly statement I made had everything to do with my ego and nothing to do with you.

These hours without you have been the worst torture imaginable. But I realise that when someone wounds you, you need time alone. I respect that. Only, don't stay away too long. Let's sort this out as quickly as possible.

My dad's back for a couple of days next week, but on Friday, I will have the house to myself. So why not ring or call round sometime during that day. I'll be in the house all day, waiting. I don't mind when you call, JUST CALL. By then a whole week will have gone by – long enough for wounds to heal – and time, surely, for us to move on.

I'm in agony here without you, Sophie. Every second without you is a wasted second.

Please, please, *call me next Friday, even if it's just to have a strop at me. I know if you don't call me, as long as I live, I won't have anything.*

I love you with my whole heart

Ben XXXX

And that, as they say, is the story so far. I peer at my watch. It's just gone half-past eight. Outside the light is draining away. My countdown is ending. So where is she? Will she suddenly appear as she did at that sixth-form party? Will she surprise me yet again? Sophie: wherever you are, I made a mistake for which I'm truly sorry. All I want now is for us to get back to normal. Do you hear me? Will you give me another chance?

What's the point of all these questions? I'm just going round and round in a circle now. I won't write any more until I know. Instead, I'll . . . I must eat. I'll cook myself something. And when you're cooking people often turn up, don't they?

0 . . . Contact is Made

It's eleven o'clock. The countdown is over. You might say contact was made.

What happened was this: I went out to the kitchen and made myself some spaghetti on toast. I sat down at the kitchen table and was just about to start eating, when the phone went. It was like a shot from a gun. I was straight up on my feet. Just hearing that phone was like a tremendous victory. When I picked up the phone I was also patting down my hair. Don't ask me why. And I said, 'Hello,' quite confidently. Everything was going to be all right, I knew it.

Then I heard a voice on the other end say, 'Ben, it's your Aunt Annie with some very good news. Your mum's had her baby, a lovely baby boy. She went into labour this afternoon and we didn't ring you before because we knew you'd be anxious.'

My mum, I loved my mum. Yet, today, I hadn't given her a second's thought.

'She is all right,' I gasped.

'Both Mum and baby are doing very well,' said my aunt. 'And you know, dear, if you want to come over tonight your uncle will pick you up . . . but I expect you're working in the video shop tomorrow morning, aren't you?'

'Yes, that's right,' I lied. Actually, I'd phoned in sick most of that week.

'Anyway, your dad will be ringing you soon, but we just wanted you to know right away. It's wonderful news, isn't it?'

'Yes, it's wonderful,' I said.

I should be there with my family rejoicing, rallying around. No wonder I felt I'd let them down.

But as soon as I put the phone down, all I could feel was this crushing, blinding disappointment. Why hadn't it been Sophie?

I rushed back into the kitchen. My spaghetti on toast was waiting for me. I heated it up in the microwave. I was hungry. But I couldn't eat it. In the end, I scraped it all away. I heard it go plonk into the bin. And I thought, what a waste. A waste of a meal. A waste of a day.

I stared at the kitchen clock, it was after nine o'clock. The waiting had gone on long enough. She had no right to drag this on any longer. How many more times did she want me to apologise? I'd rung her up, gone round to her house, written her a letter. What more could I do? Now it was her turn, surely. Just what was she up to?

I couldn't rest until I knew. I was going to call her. Enough was enough. But first, I went upstairs and put on one of her favourite tracks. I needed to attract all the good vibes I could, and she loved this song. I played the track a couple of times and that was enough to conjure her up. She was there, sitting cross-legged on my bed, smiling at something I'd said, telling me how much I'd helped her, celebrating her triumph in my play . . . We'd had so many good times. Nothing could ever wipe those out. I put the track on again, very loudly, so I'd hear it when I was downstairs ringing Sophie. I dialled the number, my hand shaking, but all those memories I'd called up had given me hope, even a little confidence.

And Sophie answered almost at once. Her tone was tired, weary but at least it was her. 'Hi, Sophie, I was just ringing to see how you were.' I was gabbling frantically, but I'd been waiting all day for this moment. There was a tiny pause and then I recoiled in horror. The way she slammed that phone down, it was like a blow right across my face.

I stood there holding on to the phone. She shouldn't have done that. I wanted to ring her up and tell her that it was my turn to get angry. Instead, I stormed about the house. Everywhere I looked there were mugs of tea, some of them were half-full, others still carried tea right up to the brim. I glared at these mugs, smugly reminding me how futile today had been. I charged around, gathering them up and threw them all into the sink. I squirted about five times too much washing-up liquid over them. There were bubbles all over the place. Next I turned the taps full on. I hadn't done that since I was about eight. I used to like the noise. Then I stood there watching the water gush over everything while tears of frustration fell down my face. Finally, I slammed the mugs away into the cupboard. I didn't want to have to see them. I stumbled back into the lounge, peering around me. I let out a howl of anguish.

Behind a pot plant lurked a mug of tea. I'm sure it wasn't there before. 'I'm not washing you up,' I screamed. Then I picked it up and smashed it against the table. Its handle immediately performed a kind of belly-flop on to the carpet, to be quickly joined by some ageing tea. I went over and started stomping on the cup, crunching it into hundreds of tiny pieces. Finally, I stopped, briefly triumphant. I'd shown it, hadn't I? I wasn't taking any prisoners today.

Still in a kind of fury, I flung the hoover out and vigorously hoovered up the cup's remains. Early this morning I'd hoovered in preparation for Sophie's arrival. Now I didn't know why I was hoovering. Finally, I sank back exhausted. I was almost grateful for the tiredness. It meant I could get out of this day soon.

And now I'm lying on my bed in the darkness. What time is it now? What does it matter? I told a girl I loved her with my whole heart. I told a girl if she didn't come back to me I wouldn't have anything. And she didn't come back. Still everything gets lost in the darkness. And we're in the darkness all the time, stumbling and groping around, seeing nothing. We never know how another person feels, not really, it's all an illusion. Until finally, the darkness swallows us up. And no one is spared. I feel oddly resigned about it now. Not upset at all.

Anticipation of death is worse than death itself. Where did I hear that? It's true, anyway. The darkness is all around me. What I'd like to do is slip under the darkness, let it carry me away with it. That's all I wish for now. Nothing else.

After-Life

30 July

I couldn't believe it. I was talking to Sophie at last. She said, 'I really wanted to come back, but in my own time, that's all.' She smiled shyly. 'I'm sorry.' I grinned at her. 'It's just good to have you back.' She shook her head. 'It's all been so silly, hasn't it?' And all at once we were laughing. We laughed and laughed. I had a pain from laughing so much until I opened my eyes.

The laughing stopped instantly. I was alone again. I lay there, bewildered by my dream. Did it mean anything? Did Sophie dream about me last night? Was it a sign? Why did I have to twist everything into a sign?

But as I drew the curtains back, I thought, a new day

and new luck. Despite the truly dire events of the last week, I still had some hope, but I couldn't stay in this house another second.

I wondered whether to go round to Simon's house. But he couldn't really help me. Sophie's sulk clearly wasn't of the 'twenty-four-hour' kind. So what was it? I wished there was someone I could consult, quite impersonally: a doctor of psychology, maybe. I wasn't sure, exactly.

In the end I went to the library. I worked through the psychology section. Most of the books were rather dry and abstract but then, tucked in between the encyclo-paedias I discovered this slim paperback devoted entirely to sulking. It was as if it had been waiting for me. I sat down and read every page of that book. And just hearing about other people's experiences seemed to dull my pain. I wished I could ring up one of these fellow-sufferers and compare notes. According to the book, sulking was a way of punishing people for emotional hurt. Well, Sophie had certainly punished me all right. It went on to explain how sulking was all to do with regaining power in a relation-ship. Was that what Sophie was doing? But I'd never thought of us in that way. I suppose I did take the lead quite a lot. But then I was rescuing Sophie, showing her a new life. And she thanked me for doing that.

Anyway, if she did think I'd been a bit pushy

occasionally, why couldn't she just have told me? It wasn't as if we didn't talk. We'd sit for hours talking about everything under the sun.

One thing the book said you must not do, is try and force someone out of a sulk. Was that my mistake? Maybe if I'd followed Simon's advice, Sophie and I would be back together now. Maybe.

When I got home Dad and Aunt Annie were waiting for me. We had a cup of tea, then they drove me to the hospital to see Mum (Glen had already visited and was now with my uncle).

My mum was sitting up in bed. To my surprise, she looked quite healthy, better than she had looked for weeks, in fact. I smiled shyly at her. 'Well done,' I said.

'Thank you, Ben.' She smiled back at me, but looked quite grave, as if this was an important moment. She leaned over and took out of the cot beside her what looked like a pile of blankets. 'And this is your new baby brother,' she said. 'We're calling him Theo, which means "gift".'

'Everyone will think he's Greek,' I observed. 'But so what.'

'You can hold him if you like,' said Mum. I leaned over. I could just make out a tiny face. Mum handed him to me. 'Just support his head, that's it,' she instructed.

I gazed down at him. He was so light, no heavier than

185

my scarf. His eyes were tightly closed. 'Is he all right?' I asked.

'He's fine,' Mum smiled. 'Remember, he's just one day old.'

'One day old, that's outrageously young,' I said.

'He reminds me of how you were,' said Mum, softly.

'I was never that little.'

'Yes, you were,' smiled Mum. 'And I've got the pictures to prove it.'

Then Dad and Aunt Annie joined us and I put Theo carefully back into his cot, so Aunt Annie could coo over him to her heart's content.

But as I was leaving Mum said to me, 'You're looking very peaky. Are you eating all right, there's lots of food in . . .'

'I'm fine,' I interrupted.

'Are you getting enough sleep?' she asked.

'When I rang him yesterday, he sounded so tense and worried,' said Aunt Annie.

Mum reached up and kissed me, then whispered, 'I'm all right, so's Theo. There's nothing to worry about.' And I could feel the tears at the back of my eyelids, because my mum was so touched that I'd been worried about her and really, I was nothing but a fraud.

On the way home Dad even got in on the act, asking me if I was working too hard in the video shop, and insisting I go round to Aunt Annie's for dinner tomorrow. He slipped me a twenty-pound note to celebrate with. The nicer he was to me, the more certain I felt that I was going to burst into tears and thoroughly shame us both.

As soon as he left, my thoughts went back to Sophie. In the end I wrote her another letter as I'd had an idea. Maybe she didn't want to talk about last week. Perhaps she knew she'd overreacted and was ashamed to talk about it now. I just told her I had to get the first draft of the play finished by the end of August and I didn't have any ideas, could she possibly help? Then I told her about Theo and how Mum would be home next Wednesday, so would she come round next Tuesday – Tuesday morning – to help me with the play.

This time I delivered it personally. I went home to wait. And I felt suddenly hopeful again. Funny how the hope kept surging back. Every hour that passed I thought, this will be the hour she comes back to me.

Tuesday, 2 August

The mystery is solved. Now I know it all. The facts are these: Sophie didn't come round on Tuesday morning. No point in dwelling on it. She just didn't turn up.

187

Nearly two weeks had gone by since I'd made that silly crack. Time enough for anyone to get over it. This time I would go round to her house, demand to see her – push my way in, if necessary – and just talk the whole thing through with her. It was just gone five o'clock when I set off. I walked briskly to her house. It was only when I was on her doorstep that I hesitated. Would Vanessa open the door? No, she'd be away with Nick now. That was a pity as I felt she was an ally. Maybe Sophie would open the door herself.

I rang the doorbell twice to show I meant business and to give myself confidence. Then I waited. My heart was thumping furiously. I made out a shape by the door. The door opened . . . and there stood Sophie's mum. Normally when I called she'd give me a tense smile. Today, she just stood there looking so hostile I was quite taken aback.

'Is Sophie there, please?' I asked.

'No, she's not,' she said firmly. 'She's gone out with Ryan.'

Ryan. For a moment I thought I was going to pass out.

'Ryan's taking her out for a meal,' added Sophie's mum. And I thought, you're enjoying telling me this, aren't you? Without even hearing my side, you hate me now. One hasty word from me and Sophie's back in

Ryan's arms and you're right beside her. No matter that I really care about Sophie, and Ryan's just using her.

Well, let Sophie find that out for herself. I've finished with her. Then I said, quite coolly, 'Thank you, will you tell Sophie I won't be calling again.' Her mum didn't know how to take that. Still, it was lucky she never saw me walk away. I moved so slowly and awkwardly it was as if I'd just been injured. But I hadn't been injured. I'd been set free. And right then I vowed to myself I would never go to that house again. And I wouldn't phone. I'd suffered my last indignity at their hands. I was leaving her to Ryan's tender mercies, for good now.

That night I invited Jenny and Simon around for a 'celebration'. 'It's all over between Sophie and me,' I announced, 'and I couldn't feel happier about it. I'm free of her at last and now I can get on with my life, which means writing my second play, seeing my first one staged at the Edinburgh Festival and having a laugh with my friends, my very good friends, Jenny and Simon.'

Simon and Jenny watched me cautiously, as if uncertain how to react. Finally, Jenny said, 'Well, up to now I've not said much about this break-up because sometimes I say things and the way it comes out isn't the way it's meant. And I knew it was a very delicate time for you, and I'm not a very delicate person.' She started to laugh, and as always, it was infectious. 'But I tell you now, when Simon told me what had happened between you two, I wasn't sorry, as I was just sick to death of Sophie. I mean, we'd go out for an evening and the whole night revolved around her. It was all Sophie, Sophie, Sophie.'

'You think I made too much of her, then?' I asked, suddenly eager to hear everything I could against Sophie.

'Oh yes, definitely,' exclaimed Jenny. 'No question there.' She looked across at Simon.

'She was a nice girl,' he said, quietly. 'That's why what she's done to you . . . I'm really shocked, actually. I did like her.'

'I liked her,' agreed Jenny. 'At first I did, anyway. And I knew you wanted to help her. So I tried to make her welcome. But then . . . it just got way over the top. Sophie was everything – nobody else mattered.'

'Oh, that's not true,' I said at once.

'Well, that's how it seemed,' said Jenny. 'Everything was for her. If Sophie had a headache, it was like, oh, what a tragedy, everyone be quiet now. And yet, when I was ill – and quite bad actually – you never even rang up to see how I was.' She smiled, 'Look, I'm not having a go at you, right?'

I smiled too. 'No, of course not.'

'But sometimes,' she said, 'I'd leave here after an evening with you, and Simon and I'd be really upset.'

'But you didn't say anything to me,' I murmured.

Jenny looked at Simon, her voice became gentler. 'I don't know why. We did talk about it, Simon and me, but you'd changed so much.'

'How had I changed?'

Her voice rose again. 'You were just a totally different person. You became very unapproachable.'

I listened to all this with a kind of fascinated horror. Here were my two closest friends telling me I'd turned into a totally different person. And they were right. Sophie had removed everyone else from my gaze.

'I feel ashamed now,' I said. Simon began to protest.

Jenny interrupted. 'You're going to hate me for saying this, but can I tell you what really annoyed me?'

'Yeah, go on.'

'The night of Sophie's party,' she paused for a moment, 'I know what Sophie told you, what I'm supposed to have said. Simon told me.'

Simon stirred a little uneasily. 'As Sophie was saying things about Jenny, I felt she had a right to know.'

'Yeah, all right,' I said, more than a little shocked that Simon had told Jenny.

'And that's how you'd changed,' said Jenny, 'believing all that rubbish Sophie said. You should know me better than that. What really happened was, I saw you shouting up the stairs at Sophie and, to be honest, I was a

191

bit embarrassed. I thought that was private, just between you and her and not for everyone to hear.'

'I was upset,' I interrupted.

'I know, darlin', I'm not getting at you. I'm just saying what I thought. So anyway, I felt sorry for Sophie. I thought you'd really put her on the spot – and embarrassed her, so I went after her, and I said, "Ben said that, because he didn't want to see you making a fool of yourself over Ryan," and she said, "Yes, I know." And then I went on, trying to be helpful, "You're really going to have to make up your mind which person you want, Ben or Ryan. You owe it to both of them to decide, finally." After which, I added, "But if it's Ryan you want it's best to say so now, even though it's going to be hard, and we will support you and still be your friends, whatever you decide . . ." '

'You had no business saying that.'

'Maybe I didn't,' said Jenny. 'But I thought, there's no good her saying, I want Ben tonight and then going off with Ryan again next week. I wanted her to make a decision, once and for all.'

'I think it would have been better if you'd stayed out of it.' I felt myself trembling.

'I wish I had now,' snapped Jenny. We stared at each other in silence for a moment.

'Still,' I said wearily, 'in a way, you were right. I

suppose I did force her to choose me that night. Anyway, she's gone running back to Ryan now.'

'And that's exactly what I was afraid would happen,' cried Jenny. 'I wanted her to make a proper choice, once and for all. I was trying to help you, and her, by calming things down a bit. But instead, she went whinging to you, saying how I was trying to push her out, when really, it was she who wanted me out of everything.'

'Do you think so?' I asked.

'Oh, she wanted the pole position in your life, no doubt about that,' said Jenny. 'I'd see her looking at me and I knew what she was thinking. I'm quite good at picking up vibes.'

'And now she's gone,' I said. And even as I said that, I felt a terrible pang of longing for her. Only the pangs kept fading in and out. One minute I wanted her, the next I was full of bitterness.

'It's hard to believe that,' said Simon. 'What she did seemed so out of character. She seemed a bit lost sometimes but she was always friendly and nice and . . .'

'You fancied her,' interrupted Jenny.

'Yes, no.' He grinned, then added, 'You and she seemed to be so happy. That's another reason, why, when things changed, we didn't feel we could say anything.'

'In a way, I was happy,' I said, slowly. 'But it was a

false happiness – a lot of hype, but nothing really. Still, it gave me a few highs.'

'Which can't be bad,' said Jenny.

'Do you know, I feel as if I've been taking a drug, a drug called Sophie. And now I'm trying to come off it and I will. You know how? By wiping out any hope that Sophie will leave Ryan and come back to me. That killer, hope, is the worst thing of all. "Tomorrow she will come back to me again." Well, she won't. It's over.' I felt myself trembling again. 'There's nothing worse than clinging on to something after it's gone, is there?'

I saw Simon and Jenny staring gravely at me. 'Don't look so serious,' I said. 'This is a good moment in my life. I'm better off without her. I'm in the real world again.'

'Welcome back,' said Jenny. 'We've missed you, because your friendship is a treasure . . .'

'Oh, shut up,' I said. 'I don't want to hear any of that waffle.'

'Right, that's it,' cried Jenny, getting up. 'And I suppose I'm disappointing, too.'

'Hugely,' I yelled.

'In that case, I'm walking out on you for ever.' She marched to the front door, then came back, grinning all over her face. 'You're supposed to run after me, try and stop me, not let me go. Come on, let's do it again.'

Instead, all three of us started to laugh at the absurdity

of it all. How ridiculously overdramatic Sophie had been. She deserved derisive, mocking laughter. That's all she would get from me in the future. I was determined to cut her out of my life, just as surely as she had cut me out of hers.

That's why I'm ending this journal about Sophie. I don't want to write about her any more or think about her any more.

She's out of my life for ever.

Friday, 2 September

I didn't think I'd be writing in this journal again, but something's happened. Something so puzzling that I need to write it down.

After Sophie broke up with me things started to go really well. I wrote the first draft of *No Returns* (it's about a boy, whom the class pick on. I'm quite pleased with it) and rehearsed *The Dreams Are Calling* for the Edinburgh Festival. I worked full-time at the video shop to earn extra money and I had my A-level results: a B and two Cs, which were just good enough to get me into Birmingham. I went out quite a lot too, often with Simon and Jenny. Jenny kept telling me about these girls who were interested in me.

'I know what you're trying to do,' I said.

'What?' she exclaimed.

I smiled grimly at her. 'Just don't tell me there are plenty more fish in the sea, all right?'

Simon started to laugh, but Jenny was indignant. 'I would never say that to you. It doesn't work anyhow. You can't just wipe someone out of your mind.'

'I don't know,' I said, bitterly. 'Some people seem to manage it.'

'No, they push things down into themselves, but they are still suffering,' said Jenny.

'So you reckon Sophie is suffering, then?'

'Oh yes.' She turned to Simon. 'Don't you?'

Simon hesitated for a moment before saying, quite sadly, 'I know what you want me to say and maybe Sophie's thinking about you at this very minute. But the awful truth is, she might not have given you a second's thought for weeks. Some people really can walk away and never look back again.'

'Really?' cried Jenny.

'I know it to be true,' said Simon, firmly.

'Who cares anyway,' I cried. 'I hardly think about her at all these days. And listen, if you ever see her walking arm-in-arm with Ryan, or someone tells you something about her, I'd rather not know, OK?'

Jenny and Simon nodded solemnly.

'Sophie is just history now.'

And then I flew to Edinburgh with Ernie and the two other cast members: Laura and Ethan. Of course they asked about Sophie. I didn't tell them any personal details. I just said she was abroad on holiday; I knew none of them believed me.

We arrived in Edinburgh around lunchtime. We checked into our hotel, had something to eat, then went to the theatre where we would be performing *The Dreams Are Calling*. We met the sponsors of the event and we chatted briefly to some of the other drama companies involved.

We were on first, at half-past six that evening. So Ernie insisted we walk all round the stage to take possession of it; apparently, Laurence Olivier used to do this.

'That's just made me more nervous,' said Laura. 'Even if I'm going to see a play the butterflies are there. Will everything go all right? But to think it's me out there.' Laura shook her head.

'I just want to get it all over with,' said Ethan. 'It's all this waiting around I can't stand.'

I ended up calming them both down. That's what's so strange now. I wasn't especially worked up.

Backstage we could hear the audience coming into the theatre. Ethan kept taking a peek at them. 'Another two rows of schoolkids just come in,' he announced.

And then we heard this woman with a heavy Scottish accent say, 'All the plays tonight are written by young people under the age of twenty-one. Our first play is *The Dreams Are Calling*, by eighteen-year-old Ben Chaplin.'

Laura whispered to me, 'Just pray I don't mess this up,' and then she and Ethan walked onstage. I listened to the lines, my lines, then came my cue. I shuffled onstage in my old man's make-up. I was frightened, yet I felt good, in control. I even remembered what Ernie had said: 'Don't do an imitation of an old man. Remember, inside, everyone stays young. That's life's real tragedy.'

I walked across the stage and switched on the video. All afternoon Ernie had been fretting there would be a problem but it came on straightaway: perfect picture, perfect sound.

For a moment all I felt was relief. Then I looked at the screen. The girl up there was so lovely: blonde-haired, enormous wide eyes . . . I'd known her once, I'd held her in my arms and her touch was always so light, almost like tickling . . . once I'd thought she loved me. Now it was as if she'd died. She was dead to me. All I had left was this ghost, saying, 'Forgetting him would be like forgetting myself.' But you have forgotten me, haven't you, Sophie?

You've gone, but still your eyes meet mine. 'I'll wait for you for ever.'

Lies, all lies.

Then I heard a voice cry, 'Sophie, I'm nothing without you, don't leave me, please.' I dimly recognised the voice as mine.

What was I doing? Those weren't my words. I struggled to get back. But then so much misery and sadness fell on to me, that all I could do was let out this great, tearing sob. The pain was crushing me. I couldn't fight it. I couldn't even cry out any more.

I just stood there in a cold sweat, staring and staring at that screen, at Sophie. Until finally she disappeared. And then I felt a ghostly hand touch mine. 'Sophie,' I gasped. I clenched her hand tightly. Then I gazed at her in amazement and disappointment. She was changing into someone else: a girl who was saying, 'She was so beautiful, Grandfather.' But I recognised this girl who was still holding my hand. It was Laura. From somewhere I found a line. That's how we carried on until the end of the scene when I stumbled away.

I stood in the wings shivering from head to toe. What had I been doing out there? It was as if something had seized hold of me, overpowered me. Ernie came over and helped me into the dressing-room. I was turning into an old man, doddering about the place. I still couldn't help shivering, not even when the play was over and Ethan and Laura were in the dressing-room too. I avoided their eyes. 'I'm so sorry,' I stuttered. Even my voice seemed to have collapsed.

'Sorry – but didn't you hear that applause?' cried Laura.

'No,' I said sadly. 'I didn't hear anything.'

Laura didn't say anything else. She just came over to me and gave me a hug and I held on to her for the longest time.

I went back to my room for a while. I felt exhausted but I didn't sleep. Later when Ernie came in to see me I asked him, 'Ernie, what happened to me tonight?'

Ernie rubbed a chubby hand over his face. 'Tonight,' he said, 'you opened a very painful door. It happens to most actors at some time.'

That made me feel a little better, as if this had been some kind of initiation ceremony into the theatre world.

'I could have sabotaged that play tonight,' I said.

'But you didn't. Instead, the audience picked up your depth of feeling. Acting's much more of a tightrope walk than people think. It's tapping emotions, yet gaining control of them too. Now me, I can turn emotions on and off. But it took time . . . I think you've learnt something tonight.'

'Yeah,' I agreed. 'Still, if it hadn't been for Laura. She was great tonight, helping me back . . .'

'That's what acting is, being part of a team, helping each other, working together.'

I knew that was a little dig at me. I'd forgotten I was part of a team. I'd just wanted to snatch the glory for myself – and Sophie. I got up and Ernie took us all out for a Mexican meal. It was surprisingly good and the mood was very friendly and relaxed.

A few days later I was sent a review of *The Dreams Are Calling*. It said the play was moving and unusual and singled out my 'deeply felt' performance. But by then I was ill in bed with exhaustion. I stayed in bed for a week. It was during that week I told Mum about Sophie and me: the whole story. I felt as though I'd regressed about ten years to when I believed my mum could solve any problem. It was oddly reassuring to do it now. And one thing I liked about Mum was she didn't make any judgements. Instead, we just chatted about all sorts of things while Theo lay watching us from his carrycot. He wasn't exactly exciting but he did fascinate me. I'd given him his bottle a few times and that day he smiled at me. Of course it could have been wind, but Mum insisted it wasn't. 'He's starting to bond with you.'

'I'm glad someone is,' I replied. After feeding Theo I sat him up and started rubbing his back. 'Do you know there's a kind of myth,' I said in a light tone, 'that our souls are flying above our heads, searching for the perfect partner and until you find your soul mate you're only half a person . . .' I hesitated, then asked in the same amused tone, 'Have you ever heard that?'

'Yes,' said Mum.

'What do you think about it?' At that moment, Theo started to burp. 'Well, that's probably the best comment on it.'

'I don't like the idea of being half a person,' said Mum. 'I think we're all complete in ourselves, but maybe we seal off part of ourselves, and certain people – not just one person – can help us to release the powers we've blocked up.'

Theo burped loudly again. 'He's certainly getting unblocked,' I said. Mum smiled. Then I said bitterly, 'The annoying thing is, for a while there I felt so good. I thought I could do anything . . . but it was fantasy. It didn't last.'

'It certainly wasn't fantasy,' said Mum. 'Maybe . . .'

'Yeah, say it.'

'I suppose the trouble with perfect relationships is they're great when they're new, but in the end what you have are human beings and when one of the partners makes a mistake – in other words acts like a human being – then they can decide it's not for them after all.'

I put Theo in his carrycot. 'It's all fantasy,' I repeated.

'I know it's very real,' said Mum gently. 'It's just

sometimes we can become so intoxicated we lose our balance.'

'And land up in the sh . . . Do you want me to change Theo's nappy then?'

'I have got you well-trained, haven't I?' said Mum. 'Are you sure?'

'Yeah, I can cope with such things, I'm safely back in the world of common sense now. And that's where I'm staying.'

It's only late at night I stray out of that world now. Last night I put Sophie on trial for crimes against me. She was standing on top of a tower in the middle of nowhere with her hair dark again and blowing about frantically in the fierce wind. My verdict was this:

'Sophie, you should carry a health warning. You're dangerous, storming out over nothing. People should know you can go funny at any minute.

'I loved you. I loved you so much I didn't belong to myself any more. But you blew it. You threw it all away. And ultimately, Sophie, you *were* a disappointment.' The wind was screaming fiercely now and Sophie gazed down at the sea far below her. Behind her stood two of my security men awaiting my orders. One push from them and she'd go hurtling into a watery grave. But I was merciful. I sentenced her to a lifetime of no one ever loving her again.

Tonight I could put Sophie on trial again. But instead I'll return to my favourite dream: the one I imagine over and over.

I'm famous and living in this massive house behind wrought-iron gates. And I'm in my study, writing my eagerly awaited thirty-fourth play, when the butler glides in. And he's just like the butlers you see in Cary Grant films. 'There's a lady to see you in the library, sir, a Miss Sophie Doyle. I took the liberty of making the young lady some tea.'

I get up slowly and permit myself a smile. She's left it far too long. Seeing her now is just an interesting diversion, an experiment in the laboratory. I'm merely curious. That's why I leave her waiting in the library, let her have a taste of her own medicine. Let her have the pain. I'm untouchable now.

More than anything, that's what I want: to be untouchable.

Wednesday, 21 September

You wait for something to happen, you hope for it with all your heart. And then when you've lost all hope . . .

Earlier this evening I'd gone out to the pictures with Simon and Jenny. It was the last time I'd see them before leaving for Birmingham early on Friday morning. So it was a special occasion. When we came back my dad was still up. We chatted to him for a while. Then he said he'd better go to bed, but he told us to enjoy ourselves and not to worry about the noise.

'My parents have been so nice to me lately,' I said.

'It's the relief that they're finally getting rid of you,' smiled Jenny.

The three of us sat around downstairs having a laugh and feeling nostalgic when the doorbell rang. It had just gone eleven o'clock and I decided it must be one of the neighbours complaining about the noise. We have the kind of neighbours who become upset if you breathe too loudly. So I opened the door, anticipating a late-night row. But instead . . .

I'd rehearsed this scene in my head a million times. Now it was real, and it caught me totally off guard.

'Can I speak to you, please?'

After nine weeks, these were the first words Sophie said to me.

'Yeah, sure, come in,' I croaked.

I opened the lounge door. It was all so normal. Simon was changing the music, Jenny was declaring, 'I'm going to make some tea, proper tea . . .' Then they saw the apparition beside me.

Jenny recovered first. 'Oh, hi, Sophie.' Even she was

oo stunned to say anything else. Sophie gave her the ghost of a smile. Then she and Simon exchanged hellos and I said, 'Come and sit down.'

'Thanks a lot,' she said.

It was all oddly formal. She sat right on the edge of one of the chairs facing the couch. She looked as if she was waiting to see the headmaster, not visiting a former soul mate. Jenny sat down on the other chair facing me, the tea forgotten, while Simon went over to the table in the corner of the room and turned around one of the chairs from there.

'We've just been to the cinema,' announced Jenny.

'Oh, what did you see?' asked Sophie.

We must have described every scene from that film. On and on, this excruciating conversation went, while my thoughts were far away. I kept sneaking glances at Sophie. She was wearing a T-shirt and jeans, very casual. Her hair had returned to its natural dark colour; in fact, she looked eerily similar to the Sophie I'd put on trial. Yet her change of hair colour also made me angry. It was like a sign that my role in her life was over. So what was she doing here? I wanted to shout at her, 'So why have you come back? What do you want with me? Why are you not with your beloved Ryan?' Yet I couldn't help feel a kind of wonderment too. For the last nine weeks she'd just lived in fragments of dreams – and on a video, speaking the words I'd written for her. But now the phantom had turned into a real person again.

Jenny threw me a glance as if to say, 'This is a bit of a shocker, isn't it?' and asked, 'Do you want us to go, Ben?'

That's exactly what I wanted. Only I didn't want it to look as if the moment Sophie arrived, I was chucking them out. After all, they were the ones who'd stood by me these past weeks. Also, I sensed Jenny didn't so much want to leave as move the conversation on. So I replied, 'No, you both stay, that's all right. Can I get you a cup of tea or something?'

'I'll make it,' said Jenny, jumping up. 'Sophie?'

'No, honestly, I'm fine,' said Sophie.

'I make better tea than Ben,' said Jenny.

'Everyone makes better tea than Ben,' smiled Simon.

Sophie was so grave and serious and ill at ease. Once she'd told me she felt more relaxed round my house than anywhere else. She certainly wasn't relaxed now. She couldn't even look me in the face tonight. Jenny returned, handing the teas out with something of a flourish. There was a tiny gleam in her eye now. 'Ben's play was a big success at Edinburgh, Sophie,' she said.

'Oh, yes, I was going to ask how that went,' said Sophie.

'Were you?' said Jenny, meaningfully. 'And he's

finished another play, *No Returns*, all on his own and it's brilliant,' continued Jenny, loyally.

'That's good,' said Sophie faintly. 'I'm pleased for you, Ben.'

But her words meant nothing. I knew that. I stared across at Sophie, sitting on the edge of her chair, with her hands locked together so tightly. What were we doing, she and I, but picking over the rubble: we were finished. Nothing was left, except the post-mortem.

'I haven't seen you for a while,' I said to Sophie. I tried to speak lightly but there was no disguising the bitterness in my voice.

'No, I've been away,' said Sophie, vaguely.

'Anywhere nice?' I asked sharply.

'Oh, just away,' she began before blurting out, 'My mum and dad have split up. My dad's in London with his new woman and my mum couldn't bear being in the house alone, so she's been staying in Sheffield with my aunt.'

I sat back at this rush of news. I wasn't altogether surprised, though. There'd been a strange atmosphere in that house, as if all the time something had to be kept at bay. What was it Sophie had said? 'My parents just tiptoe around each other, pretending.'

'So what are you doing?' asked Jenny.

'Well, I didn't want to go to Sheffield, then Nick said

he'd spoken to Vanessa and I could go with them if I liked. I just looked at him thinking, why are you being so nice to me? But I suppose I'm all the family he's got left. There's no one else now . . . And it was so lovely there in the country, right away from . . .'

'How long have you been back?' I interrupted rudely.

'Just a few days.'

'And there's no chance of your parents . . .' began Jenny.

'No chance,' said Sophie, briskly. 'He swore to my mum he wouldn't see this woman any more, that's why they went away at Easter to try and save their marriage. But then my mum found out he was still seeing her. This time she went crazy and threw him out. What a night that was.' She half-shivered, but her voice was flat and toneless. 'I don't think even my mum would take him back now. They're finished.'

It was very hard not to feel a surge of sympathy for Sophie. But I resisted firmly. 'So what else have you been doing?' My voice was cold and clinical.

She seemed puzzled. 'What else?'

I wanted to ask her about Ryan. But I couldn't bear to say his name. 'Yeah, what else have you been up to?'

She smiled faintly, staring down at the floor. 'Not a lot . . . like I said, I've been away most of the time.'

I gripped my coffee mug tightly. 'But you weren't

away when I rang you up and you slammed the phone down on me, and you weren't away when I called round and you wouldn't see me.'

'No . . . no, I wasn't away then,' her voice came out in breathless whispers.

'So why wouldn't you see me?'

'I couldn't.'

'Why?'

She looked for a moment as if she were overwhelmed by my question. I thought she was going to burst into tears. But instead, she declared, 'Because I couldn't go on being someone I wasn't. Like, you put my name on that play and I didn't write a word of it. And then I was acting in your play, and I know I can't act. All those other girls were miles better than me. It was only because of you . . .' Her voice trailed bleakly away.

'So what are you saying, that I pushed you into things?' I demanded.

'No, I wanted to do all those things. It's just you took over everything. And in the end,' her voice broke for a moment, 'I didn't know who I was any more . . . everything was going too fast. I had to have some space.'

'So why didn't you tell me this?' I cried. 'I thought I was helping you, giving you opportunities, but you didn't have to do them.'

'I know,' she said, quietly.

'So why didn't you tell me?'

'Because I didn't want to ruin our relationship.' She was almost whispering now. 'I didn't want to do anything to break us up. That meant everything to me.'

I could only laugh derisively. 'Are you sure it wasn't anything to do with Ryan?' Now I was angry enough to say his name.

'Ryan?' She sounded startled. 'I haven't seen him for months.'

'Really? What about the night I called round and your mum looked at me as if I was the Antichrist and very kindly informed me that you were out with him.'

'I told my mum to say that,' she said slowly.

'Why?' I demanded.

'Because I needed some time on my own and I knew that if you heard that . . .'

'And your mum did that. She lied for you.'

'She's very protective . . . she saw I was upset.'

'Upset,' I said, sarcastically.

'Yes,' she cried suddenly. 'Upset. What you said to me was horrible and nasty. But I knew it was true as well.'

For the first time that evening she was looking straight at me. I turned away. 'Have you any idea how horrible it is to be blocked out like that? You've given me the worst nine weeks of my life.'

'I know. I was totally wrong,' she gasped. 'Everything became so confused and . . .'

'What about my letters?' I interrupted.

'What letters?'

'I wrote to you twice, begging you to see me. How could you ignore them?'

'I don't remember . . . you see, my mum opens my letters.'

'Your mum!' exclaimed Jenny, suddenly.

'Yes, well, like I said, she's very protective. So I . . .'

'Are you saying you didn't see my letters?' I cried.

'Not right away.' Sophie's voice became muddled. 'I mean, later on I did, I think. I don't really remember.' Her voice splintered away.

'You ignored my letters,' I said quietly. 'I don't know how you could do that.'

'No,' she faltered. 'I wanted to . . .'

'Why don't you tell the truth?' yelled Simon, so suddenly he made everyone jump. He got up from the table and started glaring at Sophie. 'What are you doing round here?'

'I just wanted to see Ben,' whispered Sophie, more to herself than Simon.

But he leapt on to her answer. 'A few soft words and you think that'll make everything all right, well, it won't. It won't,' he screamed and then slammed his fist down on the television, so hard the whole room seemed to shake. I stared at Simon, alarmed but mesmerised as he ranted on: 'For no reason you just get up and leave people. One day you're just not there any more. And there's nothing anyone can do to bring you back. You got those letters all right, so why lie about it? Why? Why?' Simon stopped. He was questioning an empty chair.

I scrambled to my feet and ran to the door. I started to call her name. She was nowhere to be seen. Go after her, urged a voice in my head. You can still catch her up. Don't let her leave like this. I hesitated. But then memories started gnawing away at me: memories of the last time I'd gone after her. So instead, I just stood in the doorway, waiting. Maybe she'd come back this time. But she didn't. From far away I could hear the wail of a police siren, it just went on and on, screaming with frustration and anger and sadness.

I walked back inside. Simon and Jenny were both standing up. They looked the way people do in pubs after there's been an incident: alert, and fearful of more trouble.

'Did you catch her?' began Jenny.

'No,' I said, wearily.

They continued to stare at me. Simon looked terrible, as if he was about to pass out.

'So, what a night it's been,' said Jenny, in a rather desperate attempt at jolliness.

I stared back at her, grim-faced. Then I cried, 'I really didn't want her to go like that. It didn't help.' I was looking at Simon now. He didn't reply.

Jenny burst in, 'But she can't just come swanning back in here like the ghost of Christmas past, not after all this time. I mean, don't forget we're the ones who've seen how upset you've been. You were very near the edge for a while there. So don't have a go at us for defending you.'

'I'm not. What I'm saying . . .' I was becoming confused. 'I just didn't like her charging off like that.'

'You should have gone after her then, shouldn't you?' said Jenny snappily.

'Yes, I should,' I replied. I was still amazed at my callousness. I'd never have treated another girl in that way. I sank on to a chair, then said quietly, 'Still, it's Sophie's fault. She's taken all my niceness away.'

'Too right it's her fault,' said Jenny. 'She's the one who went all funny. And she was lying about those letters . . . that's obvious.'

'Shall we go?' said Simon abruptly. They were the first words he'd spoken since I'd come back. He looked down at me, slumped on the couch. 'I really blew it for you, didn't I?'

214

'No, no,' I began, unconvincingly. Simon was already making for the door.

'It had to be said,' interrupted Jenny. 'She's left it far too late.'

'Yeah, you're right,' I said wearily.

'I expect she thought you were going to be all over her,' said Jenny. ' "Oh, Sophie, thanks for coming back to me," all that stuff.'

'Yeah, maybe,' I murmured. 'Anyway, you two are off to a wedding tomorrow, aren't you?' I said.

'Yeah, Simon's cousin, he's a great laugh, actually. I've met him a couple of times,' said Jenny.

'Well, enjoy it and I'll give you a ring soon from sunny Brum.'

'You'd better,' said Jenny.

Our goodbyes were muted and awkward. For all my smiles and attempts at polite conversation, I still felt angry with Jenny and Simon. They'd hijacked tonight. They'd sabotaged . . . what exactly? Still, Jenny was right about one thing, Sophie had left it far too late. And anyway, running off again. Where did that get us?

Tonight, she came back to me.

But in the end she ran away again, just like before.

And she lied to me.

But she did come back.

215

Thursday, 22 September

I was up before six o'clock this morning. I crept out of the house and went for a long walk in the country. So now I knew why Sophie had run away. All night her words had come roaring back at me: 'You just took over everything . . . I had to have some space.' It was my fault, then. I'd been too demanding, too imprisoning. I'd seized all the power. But I had to: I was rescuing her. I clung desperately to that phrase. I was filling up all those spaces in her life, taking away all that emptiness. But why? For her own good? Not even I could believe that any more.

The truth was, I wanted to fill up her life so there wouldn't be room for Ryan or anyone else. Just me. I wanted every second of her life packed with me. It was quite amusing really. I started out as Sir Lancelot and ended up as the monster the heroine has to flee from. So when did the transformation take place? Was there a moment when the jealous, possessive monster took me over? Or, maybe the gap between the monster and Sir Lancelot was never as great as I thought. I didn't know. I was just disappointed in myself. But I was disappointed in Sophie too. Couldn't she at least have tried to explain what she felt? She never gave me a chance.

What did she say last night? She didn't want to ruin

our relationship. Well, she'd done that all right: she'd blown us right out of the water.

I trudged home. Mum was in the kitchen.

'You're up early.'

'Felt like a walk,' I said.

'It's lovely out, isn't it?'

I hadn't even noticed.

'As it's your last day, how about a cooked breakfast?'

'Brilliant.' I felt like eating myself silly.

'And we're taking you out for a meal tonight, so you're being thoroughly spoilt . . .' She peered through the kitchen window. 'It's such a nice day I've left Theo in the garden and Glen's playing football with James, the boy down the road. Glen's so proud that a boy who's two years older than him has asked him to play football.'

We chatted on for a while, then Mum asked, 'How did it go last night, then?' By the slight rise in her voice I knew she'd guessed something had happened last night.

'Sophie came round,' I said.

'I thought I heard her voice.' Mum sat down expectantly at the kitchen table. I recounted the highlights and lowlights of Sophie's return. I also told Mum about my surprise and anger over the way Simon had behaved.

'He was acting for the best,' said Mum.

'I'm sure he was,' I replied quickly. I felt disloyal even discussing his behaviour with Mum.

217

'I am glad Sophie came round last night,' said Mum. 'You deserved that.'

I smiled wearily. 'You make it sound as if I won a swimming trophy or something.'

'And she will call again,' Mum continued.

'What, after the reception she got last night?'

'Oh, I think she will,' said Mum. 'She must have realised it wouldn't be easy . . . Yes, she'll contact you again, one day.'

One day, that sounded horribly vague. 'You don't think I should call her myself?' I asked.

Mum looked shocked, as if the idea had never crossed her mind. It had crossed mine, more than once. But each time, I'd summoned up a memory of the last time I'd rung her, and that smothered the idea, temporarily.

'At the moment I think you both need some time, a breathing space,' said Mum. 'I'm sure she will call you again and if when you're home in the holidays you want to ring her . . . but you may find by then you've moved on. I think you already have . . . and you've got a very busy time ahead, lots of new experiences and challenges. Your dad and I are very proud of you and the way you've coped with everything.'

Of course my mum had her own angle on this: she didn't want anything to put me off my new degree course. After all, that was my future. In big capital letters. Once

I'd have mocked such a simple philosophy. Now I wondered if she wasn't right. Making something of your life: that has to be a priority.

For the rest of that morning all was frantic business. As usual, I'd left my packing to the last minute. I raced around throwing books, clothes and tapes into various suitcases. Then I went up to the shops to get a few things. But on the edges of my mind was always Sophie. I wondered what she was doing. Would she try and contact me today? Well, that was her business. I couldn't let myself be pushed into all this wondering and speculation.

The basic truth was, she'd left it far too late.

On the way back I saw a car parked outside my house. It belonged to Simon's dad. He was in the driver's seat, Simon beside him, while in the back were Jenny and David, Simon's younger brother. They were all dressed up and clearly on their way to the wedding.

As soon as Simon saw me he got out of the car, although to my surprise, Jenny didn't join him.

Simon stood in front of me in his brown suit, smiling faintly. 'I should never have said that stuff last night,' he blurted out at once. 'I was totally wrong. You see I . . .' He shook his head. He looked so uncomfortable, I couldn't stay angry with him. Most of my anger had evaporated anyway.

'Look, mate, there's no need . . .'

'Yes, there is. I owe you an explanation. You see . . .' and suddenly the words were tearing out of him, 'when my mum walked out on us I wrote to her lots of times. And I know Nan sent them on to her, but she never answered one of them, ignored them all. Then one day – well, you know – out of nowhere she turned up at our school in this big posh car, all eager to play the loving mum for a while. But I just said to her, "Why didn't you answer my letters?" and she goes, "Letters, what letters?" That's when I walked away. I knew I didn't want anything to do with her.' After that his voice started to crack. 'And I haven't thought about her for years but last night,' he grinned shyly, 'I got my wires a bit crossed. For a moment it was like she was there.' He paused.

'I completely understand,' I said.

'I've written to Sophie, I felt she deserved an explanation too,' he went on.

'Ah, but she probably won't see it,' I said. 'Her mum censors all her mail, remember.'

'Last night can't have been easy for her,' said Simon, slowly.

'The last nine weeks haven't been great for me,' I retorted, feeling suddenly defensive.

'Yeah, but she's very young, fifteen.'

'Sixteen now.'

'Whatever,' said Simon. 'I did some crazy things at fifteen, so did you.'

I looked at him closely. 'What are you saying?'

'I'm just saying that she's very young, so what we're seeing is like the undercoat, the real person comes later. I wouldn't be surprised if she's something really special in a couple of years' time.'

The car door opened and Jenny walked over to us. 'I thought you were ignoring me,' I said.

'I was trying to.' Jenny smiled. 'Actually I was being very sensitive, just for a change. I thought you two might want to talk on your own for a bit.'

'Jenny the diplomat,' I teased. 'Now I've seen everything.'

But for once Jenny was looking quite serious. 'No, we both felt we'd butted in last night. And afterwards I said to myself, just calm down, Jenny, and stop judging people. People do it to me, you know, make a judgement when they don't even know me. To be really honest, I was always a bit jealous of Sophie. Even last night I thought, there she is, stealing the limelight again. But what's gone on between you and Sophie is between you two and no one else . . . and I just want you to know whatever you decide will be all right with us.' She paused.

'You've been rehearsing saying that, haven't you?' I said.

'Too right I have,' replied Jenny. 'Apologising isn't natural, especially for someone of my calibre.'

Simon's dad sounded a polite purp on the car. 'People are always rushing me,' cried Jenny.

'Oh, but the bride and groom wouldn't dare start without you, Jenny,' I said.

'That's true,' then all at once she was enveloping me in a big hug. 'You'd better ring me soon,' she cried.

'I might, if you're lucky.'

I went to shake hands with Simon. 'Oh, give him a hug too and to be done with it,' cried Jenny. And for the first time in years, I gave Simon a bear hug too.

'We're inviting ourselves up to Brum soon,' said Simon. 'Just thought I'd let you know.'

And then after a second, less polite purp, they raced to the car. I waved them off, feeling a distinct pang of loneliness. I was really glad they'd come round to sort things out.

I went back inside and hovered by the phone. Should I ring Sophie just to say . . . I didn't know exactly. But to my surprise, I realised that part of me wanted to phone her very badly. I edged towards the phone as if it were an unexploded bomb. Why didn't I just pick up the receiver and call her? Because for all I knew she could slam the receiver down on me again and I could find myself plunged into more nightmarish events over which I had absolutely no control. Last time had been bad enough. Why invite more hassle and pain into my life? Especially when, as Mum said, I'd just sorted myself out. Besides, it was for her to ring me. If she really cared, she would try again. Why hadn't she tried again? Maybe last night had just been a whim. And she had lied about those letters. I was certain of that. Was she lying about other things? Like Ryan? I just didn't know.

It was as if between Sophie and me swirled this terrible dark fog, blurring and disguising everything. And we'd lost each other in that fog. But last night I thought I'd heard her calling to me, only the voice that rose out of the fog was muffled and distorted. I couldn't be sure what she was saying, or even if she was calling to me at all. So maybe it was best I didn't venture any deeper into the fog tonight.

I'd let her call me.

I went upstairs, finished my packing and waited for the phone to ring. When I'd finished my mum came into my bedroom. 'It's so bare now,' she said. She looked quite emotional. She added, 'You know when you come back your room will be waiting for you. This will always be your room.'

Then Aunt Annie came round. At first she was going to baby-sit with Theo and Glen. But Glen was so tearfully indignant at being excluded from this special meal, that my parents relented and decided he could come too. As a result, he was rushing excitedly around the house in his smart clothes hours before we were due to leave.

We went to a Chinese restaurant, as I'm mad about Chinese food. Glen saw me using chopsticks and was determined to have a go too. What he lacked in skill he more than made up for in determination.

He was highly amusing to watch. A real floor show. And soon it seemed the whole restaurant was laughing at his antics. I was pleased to have the attention distracted away from me as, for once, I hardly ate anything.

I was too busy wishing I'd rung Sophie.

The arguments inside my head had stopped. What did it matter who was right and who was wrong?

Even the pain I'd felt when she walked out on me had turned into a tribute to her: only someone very special could make me miss her so much.

In the end all that mattered was this: I'd buried Sophie deep inside me. I'd buried her so deeply I thought I'd lost her. Something in me did turn sour, leaving me feeling hollow, empty. At the time that seemed a kind of victory; a regaining of power. But I hadn't lost Sophie at all. Everything I'd felt for her was still there inside me. I'd never lose her. But was that my triumph or my tragedy? I didn't know. I just knew I had to ring her.

It was after ten o'clock when we arrived home. Dad

carried Glen upstairs. Mum followed him and I heard her whispering to Aunt Annie. This was my chance to ring Sophie. My last chance. So why was I hesitating? I was scared, scared she'd slam the phone down on me. But I had to take that risk. There was no other choice. I reached out for the receiver and as I did so it started to ring. I stared at it in amazement, then I snatched it up. Somehow, I knew . . . it had to be . . .

'Hello,' I said.

'You're back.' Sophie sounded breathless as if she'd been running.

'Have you rung before, then?' I asked.

'A couple of times.'

'Oh, I'm sorry, I've been out. My family took me for a farewell meal. I'm off first thing tomorrow.'

'Tomorrow.' She sounded shocked. 'As soon as that.'

'Yeah, I've got fresher events first. You know, where they try and get you to join the society for the prevention of cruelty to traffic cones.'

'Best of luck, Ben. I know you'll do well,' she said, then she added, confidingly, 'I've just enrolled at college for three A levels, including drama.'

'That's good. You'll have to let me know when you're acting in something.'

'Don't hold your breath. I am really pleased your play went well in Edinburgh. I often thought about it.'

tually, you were there, a part of it.'

'as I?' Her voice was now very faint. There was a pause.

I was uncertain how to go on. 'I'm sorry about your family. I mean about your mum and dad breaking up.'

'It had to happen. In a way it's better now.'

There was another pause until I said, 'Simon has written you a letter to apologise for what he said last night.'

'He didn't need to do that. I deserved it. It was true. I was totally wrong in what I did.'

'No, you weren't,' I said quickly. 'I made mistakes, huge mistakes. You had to do what you did. I got so intense about everything and I pushed things far too much. We were going along there at about a thousand miles an hour. If we'd gone on much longer we'd have probably got married or something.'

Sophie gave a muffled laugh, then cried, 'I did get your letters. I lied. They're here beside me now, I've read them over and over.'

'But you didn't answer them,' I said.

'No . . . I didn't answer them.' Her voice started to shake. 'I couldn't, Ben. I tried. Every day I was away from you I missed you so much, but I had to go away . . . my mum and dad made such a mess of everything and then I made a big mistake going out with Ryan and then, there you were, and it was wonderful, but it overwhelmed me. I wanted to be sure I was ready for it all, and by the time I knew, it was too late. I couldn't just go round and see you after the way I'd messed everything up. But do you know what I did? I went to the top of Windmill Hill. I thought I could talk to you there, and every night I looked for you, but I never saw you.'

'You wouldn't. I stopped going there after we . . .'

'That explains it then,' said Sophie. Somehow, that sounded funny. We both tried to laugh.

'And then last night,' continued Sophie, 'I thought this is so stupid, sitting on top of this hill, waiting. So I went to your house, spent an hour hovering around outside and finally . . . I've left it far too late, haven't I?'

'No, you haven't,' I cried, 'because, coincidentally, I'm off to Windmill Hill right now. So if you . . .'

'I'll be there,' cried Sophie at once.

'I'll be round your house in five minutes then.' My voice was all over the place now. 'That's if you're not in your pale blue nightie or anything.'

She laughed shakily. 'No, no.'

'I'll see you soon then. Sophie, are you still there?'

'Yes, I'm here.'

'You're the best.'

'So are . . .' she began, but then whispered, 'I love you, Ben.'

'While we're changing lines here,' I croaked, 'I love

you so much . . . and now I'm going to put the phone down because I can't wait another second to see you.'

SOPHIE! SOPHIE! SOPHIE! The word danced and whirled around my head.

Now through the fog blazed a light. The most wonderful light. And right then I knew I was going to follow that light, no matter where it led me. This was one trail that would never end.